"Alpha Tango Three to Alpha Tango Two."

There was no reply, and Gadgets Schwarz knew from the manner in which static was now coming from the portable radio in weak sputters—instead of a steady hiss—that the battery's power had been seriously drained. It probably hadn't been recharged in days. He also knew that he had nobody but himself to blame for that.

"Alpha Tango Three to Alpha Tango Two," he repeated. This time there wasn't even any static.

The pak-set's battery was dead.

"Damn," he muttered under his breath.

He was about to repack the radio when a twig snapped behind him and the swirl of fight-or-flee adrenaline flooded his gut.

Schwarz had no time to do either. Someone had placed the barrel of a pistol against the base of his skull and pulled back the weapon's hammer with a sickening *click*!

"Able Team will go anywhere, do anything, in order to complete their mission."
—*West Coast Review of Books*

Mack Bolan's

ABLE TEAM®

ABLE TEAM.

Night Heat

Dick Stivers

A GOLD EAGLE BOOK FROM

WORLDWIDE.

TORONTO • NEW YORK • LONDON • PARIS
AMSTERDAM • STOCKHOLM • HAMBURG
ATHENS • MILAN • TOKYO • SYDNEY

First edition October 1989

ISBN 0-373-61244-3

Special thanks and acknowledgment to
Nicholas Cain for his contribution to this work.

Printed in U.S.A.

PROLOGUE

The scorpion had backbone. Tail curled into the striking position, it jabbed at Rosario Blancanales's boot several times before scurrying about in angry circles and striking once again. From his position at the open side of the Border Patrol van where he watched the agents check their weapons, Rosario kicked the fist-size scorpion out into the night. He was intrigued by the revolting creature's tenacity—its courage at tangling with someone so much larger without complaint.

"Your bravery saves you from a squashed destiny," the Able Team commando said as he watched the scorpion tumble end over end through an abandoned spiderweb, landing on its back in the dust. Quickly righting itself, the deadly arachnid scurried off through clumps of cactus.

"Say again, buddy?" one of the agents asked, glancing back over a shoulder.

"Aw, nothing," Blancanales replied leaning out the van. "I was just admiring some of your native inhabitants—bad dudes of the eight-legged variety."

The border patrolman followed his gaze. "Yeah, they're feisty little bastards," he said. "But not half as bad as a Gila monster that's found its way into your sleeping bag."

"Gila monster?" Blancanales swallowed hard, shifting on the torn canvas seat. His eyes darted about to make sure he was still alone in the vehicle. "You mean one of those..."

"Fat, ugly, beady-skinned lizards. Heavy as possum, but more sluggish—with one righteously nasty disposition"

"The only poisonous lizard in the *U*-nited States," another agent, who had overheard their conversation joined in.

"They're lazy and slow, but once they clamp onto you, they never let go. You can kiss it goodbye, brother, once they gotcha!"

Blancanales jumped as a border patrolman lurking on the other side of the van reached through and pinched his leg, much to the amusement of everyone clad in brown and green calico.

"They just kinda grind away at the flesh, slowly chewing, injecting poison with each bite."

"Just about takes major surgery to get 'em off."

"Decapitation. It's the only remedy."

"Shit . . ." Blancanales's eyes shifted skyward as a falling star dropped low in the brilliant heavens, disappearing beyond an orange crescent moon.

"Let's get this show on the road!" A stocky supervisor strutted past, tapping torsos to ensure each man was wearing his bulletproof vest.

Blancanales had heard that border patrolmen usually didn't bother with body armor, but tonight theirs was a special mission—a task that invited gunplay, dared Lady Death. It wasn't all that inconceivable that a couple of them might not be among the living at the predawn head count.

Engine off and lights out, the van sat on a narrow dirt road at the edge of a box canyon's sheer cliff walls. The escarpment dropped four or five hundred feet to several interlocking mesas and a vast, slanting plateau. The canyon itself was a narrow, mile-long gouge in the endless rolling hills of cacti and sagebrush that separated Mexico from the United States. It was "a rock's throw" from El Paso, as the *pollos*, or illegal aliens, called it.

There was no reinforced chain link here, no concrete barriers preventing, or slowing, the "brown hordes" from crossing into the Land of Dreams. No sagging coils of barbed wire, or buried intruder detection devices. Just a dilapidated series of broken fence posts—many all but buried in the sand—from which rusting strands of cut and broken wire curled like slumbering rattlesnake tails. Here the sagging line of barbed wire tumbled down rolling hills into virtually impassable terrain—at least for any vehicle that wasn't equipped with four-wheel drive. The incline ended in Canine Canyon, aptly named because of the running packs of wild dogs that inhabited it. The canyon, a series of dry gulches, many a hundred yards wide and twice that deep, was also known as Dead Man's Zone.

The Immigration and Naturalization Service—INS—sent its mandatory repair crew out every week or so, but little money or command concern was funneled into this stretch of barren badlands. It just wasn't worth the effort. The illegals swarmed through the canyon every night, only to be turned back by a particularly vicious stretch of the Rio Bravo located farther inland—turned back to Mexican territory, where they would divert south toward San Elizario. The *pollos* never learned—at least not the first-timers. Perhaps the human coyotes, or guides, led them through the high, inescapable walls of Canine Canyon because the illegals were so unsuspecting...so vulnerable. It was where the coyotes had taken to beating and robbing their human cargo—killing a few *pollos* now and then, or raping an attractive *pollita*. It was a natural slayground, a traditional battlefield where a thousand Indians and U.S. Cavalry soldiers had died more than a hundred years earlier...a haunted land that the locals avoided because of the eerie legends and curses associated with it.

None of these things really occupied the thoughts of Blancanales or the other men in his patrol. The Border Patrol rarely assigned a whole vanload of armed anti-intruder specialists to Canine Canyon. But tonight was different. The entire week had seen an unprecedented flurry of honcho activity billowing forth from the El Paso office.

The warning from Washington had gone out: terrorists with alleged Libyan connections were at it again, trying to smuggle suitcase nukes or surface-to-air, shoulder-launched rockets into America via the Mexican border. It was possible that another assassination attempt on the President was planned, or the sabotage of a nuclear reactor. The particulars didn't matter to Rosario "Politician" Blancanales or the team he'd been assigned to work with. The important thing was that they knew and understood that the foreign agents they'd been sent to intercept would be heavily armed and most probably of the suicide commando mentality. The mission wasn't to be taken lightly.

The men Blancanales was working alongside were all veterans with five or more years of border surveillance under their belts. But none of the officers had ever come in contact with a bona fide Communist agent in the line of duty—only dirty, grimy *pollos* seeking a bit of the "good life" on the other side. And they didn't think tonight would be any different.

"Gonna be a prick-freezer out here tonight," one of the youngest border patrolmen muttered, rubbing his hands together roughly, then reaching for a portable stove secreted beneath a bench seat in the van.

"Don't touch that sucker, Garcia!" a tall barrel-chested supervisor with close-cropped gray hair and thick black glasses whispered harshly. His teeth were clenched around a cigar stub that glowed brighter with each excited breath. "The wetbacks'll see the gas flame from two miles off!"

"Hell, that's what I was hoping for," the youngster muttered. "Flames mean heat. It'll attract 'em. Then we can get some action stirred up, Pat. Otherwise we're gonna be pullin' on our puds out here all night, freezin' off our gonads. I got a love life to worry about, you know."

"Hmph," the supervisor said, clearing his throat as he reached into the van to turn the gas stove off before low man on the totem pole could light it.

"Ain't nobody out there tonight, Chief," one of the older patrolmen decided as he scanned the shifting black lines and shadows with a pair of folding binoculars. "Nobody but scorpions and rattlers." In the distance a pack of wild dogs took up a lonely chorus of wails, yelps and whimpers. "And coyotes," the veteran *pollo* wrangler added.

With detached indifference, Blancanales surveyed the antics of the border patrolmen. He was well aware they were hardened, street-educated pros who knew their craft much like any wizened city cop. A year guarding the nation's invisible boundary, dodging rocks, bricks and other hand-thrown missiles from the Mexican side, had made them a close unit. He knew the horseplay he'd just witnessed was essential to their sanity.

Their antics reminded him of his colleague Carl Lyons, and an incident the Ironman had relayed to him not long ago about his old LAPD days. It had been a quiet, uneventful Sunday night, and five of the district units were cruising the ghetto, car lights out, playing cat and mouse with one another. Three men would hide behind warehouse dumpsters or down dark alleyways. The other two would seek them out. Hide-and-seek, big-league style. There was no tag involved, however. When a black-and-white was spotted, the "hunter" shot at the emergency roof lights with an air gun. Lyons's pellet pistol had held an unusually powerful dose of carbon dioxide in the chamber that night; its high-velocity projectile had shattered his buddy's windshield. They had been forced to radio a bogus sniper call to account for the damage. In the ghetto, radio air traffic concerning a rooftop rifleman was no big thing. One of the other patrolmen broadcast a Code-4/Gunman GOA—gone on arrival—within seconds of the less than genuine call for help. Not a single district sergeant responded. Snipers in Watts had been routine in the seventies.

"He looks like he's thinking about some woman," one of the border patrolmen commented, finally bringing Blancanales into the conversation.

Taking his cue, the Able Team commando chuckled. He nodded and said, "Yeah, I'd much rather be home cuddling some babe than out here warming the fossils with *you* clowns."

"Ain't that the everlovin' truth," a different patrolman said, laughing loudly. The others joined in with insults, private little jokes and brief reminiscences of better times, notably day shift assignments, where one was off by 1400 hours and could spend the night with the best-looking woman at the local cop bar.

Blancanales's grin seemed plastic, contrived, however. In reality he hadn't been with a woman in months. The job prevented that. Able Team. It was a covert antiterrorist squad called into action by none other than the President. Lyons and Schwarz and that crazy man, Hal Brognola, too. Always the job. Always some dilemma threatening the country that only the men of Stony Man Farm—the group's control central in the Blue Ridge Mountains of Virginia—seemed able to combat. In a way, he had become used to the hassles of paramilitary life—to putting the homeland first, keeping personal problems a secondary concern. Love lives for men like Blancanales were a luxury. Sometimes he felt he just didn't need the extra headaches anyway.

Blancanales liked to believe that his sentiments leaned in that cynical direction, but in reality he cherished the few personal relationships he had developed. He loved life despite the warrior's code he lived by and the knowledge that the next mission might deliver him to his doom.

He knew from experience that the men who were aware they might die during the next chopper flight into danger's threshold made the best soldiers. They either knew no fear, or had been trained to control it. If they lost control, they were prepared to step into the next life, content with and resolved to their fate.

"I'm putting in for a transfer to San Diego," one border patrolman threatened good-naturedly as he glanced over at their supervisor.

"Hell," another trooper said, smirking. "San Diego wouldn't have you. El Paso's the end of the line, doofus. Face facts, *pareja*. You're stuck with Texas, and we're stuck with you."

Pareja. Partner. That brought another round of restrained, almost cautious laughter, and Blancanales joined in, feeling the sudden need to belong, to be accepted by these men who courted death nightly on America's southwest frontier.

The barely audible drone of a propeller-driven airplane jolted Blancanales's attention to the mission at hand. Laughter forgotten, his soldier's instincts took over. The moon had faded from view along the horizon, and the desert haze obscured whatever starlight might have assisted in locating the spotter plane's outline against the black sky. Blancanales scanned the heavens but knew he would see no navigational lights. He turned and motioned to Robert Patterson, the senior border patrolman who was crouched between a mint-green Ford van and an International truck. But Patterson was more concerned with the movement he'd just detected along the rim of the canyon.

Shapes in the dark. Eight or nine of them. Bent low to the ground, reminding Blancanales of VC sappers sneaking up on the U.S. embassy in Saigon, more than twenty years earlier.

Funny how mental images could remain so sharp even two decades later.

And, like that terrible night so long ago in Vietnam, it appeared that one of these intruders was carrying a rocket launcher on his shoulder.

1

Less than a mile southeast of Canine Canyon, Rosario Blancanales's two Able Team colleagues were lying on their bellies in an underground sewage tunnel, swatting at mosquitoes and squinting at the shifting shadows of the night.

Constructed of concrete and brick, the tunnel passed beneath a pyramid-shaped hill separating the United States from Mexico. It had been built over fifty years earlier and was badly in need of repair. Raw sewage collected in murky puddles all around Carl Lyons and Hermann Schwarz. Rats the size of small alley cats prowled the shadows, often refusing to flee when the Ironman or Gadgets flung a chip of concrete or broken bottle in their direction.

These were hard core rodents—wetback rats from the Mexican side, Gadgets joked. Gadgets Schwarz, the electronics wizard of the group, half expected to see one of the fanged predators put on a sombrero in brazen defiance— that was how confident these smelly tunnel monsters were. Lyons, the ex-cop and resident Shotokan karate expert, had to agree with his current partner on that count: these rats were *bad* characters. Their eyes glowed red and sometimes green in the pitch-black, depending on the degree of starlight or natural phosphorescence or mushroom glow affecting their already eerie surroundings. The rats hissed each time Lyons or Schwarz or one of the three border patrolmen with them on the stakeout moved so much as a muscle.

Rats weren't the only dangers confronting the two men. There were spiders and snakes and other creepy-crawlers that dangled from the tunnel's web-lined ceiling. The tunnel couldn't have been more than three feet in diameter, which meant the ceiling was only mere inches above their heads.

There were also scorpions. Gadgets Schwarz had never seen so many of the pink and blue creatures scurrying about at one time, and that included during his time spent in Nam *and* boot camp, where it was common knowledge that drill sergeants imported any number of exotic creatures to torment and terrify their green recruits.

Rats, scorpions and hairy fist-size spiders weren't the primary opponents tonight, however. There was a far more deadly menace lurking in the dark Mexican night.

Coyotes. Predators of the two-legged variety, worse than the mythical werewolves of Transylvanian legend and the silver-screen—for they were often armed to the teeth with firearms that discharged real lead. And not of the silver bullet persuasion, but hollowpoints, or full-metal jackets.

Lyons and Schwarz had been assigned to "curtail" the activities of Mexican nationals who prowled the seldom-watched and sparsely guarded tracts of borderland, waiting for small, defenseless groups of *pollos* to cross illegally into Texas. Unlike the routine coyote, whose "services" included escorting undocumented workers across the border without observing the usual immigration requirements, two particularly vicious coyotes had taken to beating and robbing the *pollos* and raping their women.

Sentiment for the illegal aliens' plight wasn't easy to come by, of course. Letters sent to editors of the many newspapers serving the region claimed that the wetbacks were only getting what they deserved—and at the hands of their own people, no less!

Until the Vasquez sisters made the headlines. They were nine-year-old twins whose parents had been killed in

Ciudad Juárez a few months earlier. Nothing dramatic: it was during the rainy seasons, when roads were worse than usual. A bus went off some cliff, crashed down a thousand-foot embankment, exploded into flames and burned all the passengers to a crisp. In addition to the parents of the Vasquez girls, forty-four other people died.

Although unusual in a country where families are often large and interrelated, the Vasquez sisters had no cousins, aunts or uncles to take them in. It made the tragedy doubly difficult for social workers to contend with. So the young girls chose to make the fabled trek to the land of lights and easy opportunity—Hollywood.

They got no farther than Canine Canyon, of course. That was where the dreaded bandits struck. The coyotes. On the American side. A scant few feet from the dilapidated barbed wire fence.

Nine-year-old twins. Beaten and gang-raped and finally killed. The newspapers had a field day. The Border Patrol and the county sheriff and anyone else wearing a uniform was criticized, chastised and just about crucified.

Insiders knew it wasn't the fault of any American peace officers. Eyewitnesses and evidence at the scene pointed to none other than *judiciales*—Mexican policemen. Or somebody posing as *judiciales*. Lyons prayed it was the latter. He knew Mexican officers could be horribly corrupt, but in the back of his mind a cop was a cop was a cop. Lyons didn't want to think he was hunting a "brother," whether Mexican *or* American.

Canine Canyon was becoming one big migraine for the brass. First, terrorists headed their way, and now child molesters infesting the often invisible perimeter.

The El Paso office of the United States Border Patrol hoped to kill two vultures with one grenade on this project.

Lyons and Schwarz weren't dressed like officers of the law. They weren't clad in commando gear, or even coveralls belonging to the Border Patrol. Tonight the two Able Team heroes were imitating *pollos*. Illegal aliens.

They wore tennis shoes flapping open at the toes, close-cropped hair hidden beneath bandanas or rolled-up ski masks, and two or three layers of dark makeup to conceal their pale skin. Their clothes were old, torn and dirty, and also worn in layers—genuine *pollos* always wore two layers of clothing, minimum, so that the outer one could be shed once they reached new jobs on American soil. *Pollos* traveled light.

But no real coyote would think them genuine wetbacks, sneaking across the border in the dead of night, hoofing it north, toward the land of opportunity. No way, José. Their voices would give them away. And, long before that, their features would announce that five Americans, not Mexican nationals, were lying there in that sewer tunnel beneath the hill in El Paso's Dead Man's Zone. And that could prove deadly.

Lyons was six foot two and just an ounce or two over 190 pounds. His blond hair was kept short and had only a few strands of gray in it. His eyes were ice-cold blue, and hard to impress. A former college football lineman, he was the biggest of the Able Team trio. Though the commandos carried only rifles on tonight's mission, Lyons was partial to a Colt Python .357 Magnum with eight-inch barrel, complete with ventilated rib.

The man sharing the luxurious quarters beside him, Hermann Schwarz, preferred the nickname "Gadgets." He was a couple of inches shorter and probably twenty-five pounds lighter than Ironman but no less a night raider and street fighter. He, too, had blue eyes and was sporting his usual trademark mustache this week, though a little bushier than usual—due, no doubt, to their extended forays into Dead Man's Zone. Though Gadgets was good with anything that could discharge hot lead, he preferred to go into combat with a silencer-equipped 9 mm Beretta 93-R.

The makeup Schwarz and Lyons had donned tonight wasn't designed to fool anyone—it was only an attempt to buy some time. They hoped it would help them lure some coyotes in close enough so that Lyons and Schwarz and their new Border Patrol buddies could pounce.

They were after the scum who had taken to robbing defenseless border crossers... the bandits who masqueraded as "guides" but pulled blades or guns or baseball bats once they'd entered that stretch of real estate between Mexico and the United States that neither government wanted to claim.

Hopefully their quarry would include the men who were impersonating *judiciales* and mutilating young girls who hadn't even succeeded in reaching their teens.

Lyons and his people were armed to the proverbial teeth with short-barreled assault rifles that resembled M-16s with shrunken stocks and extended flash suppressors. The CAR-15s were composed of blue steel and black fiberglass and carried 30-round banana clips. Each man also toted four extra 20-round magazines in dual ammo pouches hanging below his parka.

The Vasquez sisters had been hacked to death with machetes, but witnesses claimed two of the coyotes brandished what appeared to be Thompson submachine guns— the kind often used by old-style gangsters. They apparently had a round drum of bullets attached to them. Lyons had seen what a burst of Thompson .45 slugs could do on the firing range, as well as in real life on the street. Tonight—as on most nights in the recent past—he wore no bulletproof vest, and the thought sent a shiver through him as he recalled the grizzly wounds on display at his first Thompson .45 shoot-out scene.

Like most mob hits, it hadn't been a pretty picture, although nearly every news rag in Los Angeles had splashed several angles of the back-alley carnage across their front pages for three days in a row.

Tonight Carl Lyons felt the group's luck would change. Something in the air, mixed with the gut instinct that had been gnawing at him for the past two hours, encouraged the Able Team commando. A twig snapping in the distance further reinforced this feeling.

"Did you guys hear that?" Gadgets Schwarz whispered softly.

"Shut up!" Lyons spat back.

"I heard it," one of the border patrolmen responded softly.

"Me, too," another patrolman whispered. "Down that gully there," he said pointing uselessly, given the darkness.

But all eyes followed the blur of movement. They knew the spot he was talking about. They'd all heard the noises— or thought they had.

This was the first night of the team's projected two-week stakeout program in that particular part of Dead Man's Zone, but the five hours they had already spent huddled in the tunnel had seemed like five entire shifts.

Now the prospect of some action shifted their adrenaline pumps into overdrive.

"Everybody keep cool," Lyons reminded. "Might just be another wild dog."

"Patience, my butt," the border patrolman nearest Ironman replied. "If it is, he gets smoked."

"Who's in *charge* of this operation, anyway?" another border patrolman asked, the irritation in his tone obvious.

"Sorry," Lyons said, forcing the word out. "Just hold on to your gonads, okay? I want to make sure—"

But further caution was unnecessary. It was a group of Mexicans. *Pollos.* Judging by hair length and the outline of some skirts in the darkness, Lyons judged three men, three women and two children. A young group: they were moving quickly through the debris littering the broken-down fence line. Then one of the young women giggled suddenly and stumbled.

"Sshhh!" Lyons heard the *pollo* in charge reprimand his wife, sister or girlfriend with a low hiss. In Spanish he said, "We're close to the checkpoint now! Be quiet!"

"*Sí,*" the woman shot back, her tone telling the man she thought he was overreacting.

"They're just a family of illegals," Schwarz whispered to the men lying behind him.

"I want you to know that it's hard as hell for me to just lie here and do nothing while those criminals walk by twenty feet in front of my nose," one of the border patrolmen whispered back. But his tone told Schwarz and his partner that he was probably grinning as he spoke.

"We're waiting for the big fish," Lyons reminded him unnecessarily. "The *banditos*. A handful of wetbacks won't get you no press, bud. On the other hand, the arrest of the notorious Dead Man's Zone coyotes would probably get you a promotion."

The *pollos* froze, and Lyons gritted his teeth: they were doing too much talking.

But it was quickly evident that the *pollos* hadn't detected the American peace officers hiding at the tunnel's mouth. Rocks began rolling down from the hilltop as five men brandishing machetes appeared overhead.

A gasp escaped one of the women as the Mexican bandits rushed down the hillside. They slid through the clumps of cacti and scrub oak like matadors eager to confront the bull, and surrounded them.

"Where are you headed?" one of the bandits demanded in Spanish.

"El Paso," one of the male *pollos* replied meekly.

"You'll need a guide," the bandit said, slapping his knee gently with the flat side of his long blade. It glistened in the starlight, and one of the women crossed herself. *La Migra* is everywhere," he warned, reminding them of the immigration authorities.

"We have very little money," the *pollo* replied.

"We can escort you across the border into El Paso for twenty U.S. dollars a head," the bandit leader returned, his tone starting to grow impatient.

"Twenty dollars?" the *pollo* leader gasped. "We don't have that kind of money, *señor*!"

"It doesn't have to be money," came the terse reply. "You have jewelry, perhaps? Bullion or—"

"We are already *across* the border!" one of the women bravely interrupted him. She gestured back toward the dilapidated fence line the group had just crossed.

"Shut up, woman!" the *pollo* leader reprimanded. He knew the rules of this wretched game. It was a game of death, and violating the code of machismo by insulting the bandits who were blocking their path could result in a heavy penalty. It was the women who would end up being violated. These bandits were armed with long machetes that had most probably spilled blood in the past. And none of the *pollos* were armed.

The gang leader laughed loudly. He threw his head back and laughed again. *"She!"* he said, waving his long, gleaming blade in the direction of the female voice. "She will be the first one we teach manners to tonight!"

And the game was over. There would be no more bargaining. Even if one of the *pollos* were to suddenly produce a treasure chest of gold bars, the fate of the woman with the brazen attitude was already sealed.

The bandits started toward her, and the other two women fled into the darkness, racing back toward Mexico. There was no screaming—only panting, the sound of dresses and soft-soled shoes rushing through the mesquite, elbows striking elbows as the *pollos* tried to scatter like birds rising before a shotgun blast.

"Let's go!" Lyons shouted.

The bandits already had the brazen woman down and were pinning her arms to her sides, ripping her three layers of garments from her body.

"*¡Policía!*" one of the border patrolmen yelled as Schwarz, Lyons and the other men rushed toward the scene, the powerful flashlights taped to their rifle barrels suddenly casting bright beams of silver to and fro as the officers zigzagged into the melee.

"*¡Policía!*" the border patrolman repeated as they towered over two of the bandits, who were attempting to commit a sexual assault on the defenseless woman. Both men glanced back at the group of wild-eyed Americans dressed like bums, and produced amused expressions rather than the raised hands Lyons had been hoping for.

"You must wait your turn, *amigo!*" the ringleader said, switching to English, mistaking the Americans for homeless bush vets or escaped convicts, but certainly not police officers or border patrolmen.

Lyons was quickly losing patience. He grabbed a handful of hair and jerked the would-be rapist back onto his haunches, while Schwarz buttstroked the other bandit with his CAR-15, and the border patrolmen disarmed the coyote brandishing the machete.

Swiftly rolling the prisoner over onto his belly, forcing his arms behind his back and snapping flexi-cuffs around the bandit's wrists, Ironman directed two of the border patrolmen to apprehend the lone Mexican who was chasing one of the other women back over the border.

When they hesitated, he yelled, "Watch him!" He motioned toward his immobilized prisoner only once, then sprinted off into the night toward the sound of a struggle fifty yards distant.

When Lyons finally reached them, the bandit was on his knees, groaning. The *pollita* had been determined not to surrender without a fight, and a well-placed kick to the groin had served to rupture any sexual desires the coyote had harbored. The woman now stood over him, hands on her hips, mouth set firmly and unforgivingly as she prepared to bring a knee up against the man's nose.

She glanced up, saw Lyons running toward her with a rifle in his hands and brought the knee up anyway.

His nasal bones smashed flat, the coyote flopped backward. He was out cold, and the woman was already whirling to flee again when Lyons latched onto her wrist.

She responded with a flurry of dainty punches, which continued a full ten seconds after Lyons identified himself both in English and Spanish. Finally her trembling fists dropped. *"¿Policía?"* Her eyes rose to lock onto his. "Really?"

"Yes, really," Ironman confirmed, bringing his bruised and scarred knuckles up slowly. He wiped the tears from her cheeks before she embraced him and broke down into an endless stream of sobs.

"Shit." He sighed, feeling his face redden. Lyons was looking down at a young woman in her late teens or early twenties. She was slender and attractive despite her disheveled appearance, and her long black hair dropped to a trim waist.

After a few moments of catching her breath, she looked up at him again. Lower lip trembling, she said, *"Gracias, señor."*

"Let's go back," he told her. *"La Migra* will want to talk to you."

"Then I will be deported," she moaned.

"Yes." His eyes darted from American soil to the Mexican side, then back again. He released her arms. "Why don't you go on back, on your own?"

"Into Mexico?" she asked, her voice cracking.

"Yes. I'll tell them you got away." He dropped to one knee beside the groaning coyote and began fastening another pair of flexi-cuffs onto the man's wrists.

"I would not know where to go," she said, eyes downcast now.

"What?" Lyons glanced up.

"I am not Mexican," the woman revealed. "I am Salvadoran. I have no place to go. I will go with *La Migra*," she said, starting back toward the border patrolmen. "It is not a great inconvenience. We have walked for three months. After *La Migra* lectures us and takes us back over the border, we can cross again. I only hope that they do not take us all the way to Tapachula before releasing us . . ."

Lyons knew she was talking about the Mexican border with Guatemala. "Yes . . ." he whispered.

"Then I would have to walk another month or two before reaching El Paso again."

Lyons fought the urge to big-brother the woman as he jerked the semiconscious bandit to his feet and started dragging the man back to the scene of the attempted rape. "After what I saw here tonight, something tells me you'll be all right."

"We will probably be turned over to the authorities in my country. Salvadoran secret police will take us away. We will . . . disappear."

"The death squads have been . . . disbanded," Lyons argued, frowning. "And that's *if* they ever really existed."

The woman laughed. "Perhaps you could find it in your heart to sponsor me, *señor*."

Lyons's own laugh was not nearly so plastic. He realized how young she really was as the Border Patrol helicopter passed overhead, and its brilliant spotlight lit up the gully. She was probably eighteen, maybe seventeen. The instinct to protect was very strong.

"Good job, dude," Schwarz congratulated, interrupting Lyons's thoughts. Three Border Patrol Jeeps bounced down the hillside and skidded up to the scene, their headlight beams playing across the crestfallen faces of the arrested *banditos*.

"We lucked out," Lyons replied dryly, his eyes remaining focused on the young woman. Standing thirty feet away, a swirling twister of dust between them as additional Jeeps arrived, she stared back, nodding, a shy, innocent smile in place, telling him she understood that he could offer no sanctuary.

Maybe another time, Ironman, he thought, listening to the echo of voices laughing inside his head, taunting. Another tour of duty...

"Well-done," a Border Patrol supervisor said as he shook the Able Team warrior's hand. "We been after these guys for months, and you cowboys got 'em in one lousy night!"

"Luck rode the wind with us tonight," Lyons muttered, turning away.

"What was that, son?"

"Oh, nothing."

"I'm going to put you boys in for a commendation," the supervisor said, his chest expanding importantly, cheeks filling to compete with the ear-to-ear grin. "Going to telex your bosses at the Pentagon or wherever, make sure they know what genuine hot dogs you turned out to be."

"Appreciate it," Lyons mumbled, but he was no longer listening.

"Got to admit I was skeptical at first..."

Lyons was walking away now toward one of the Border Patrol Jeeps. He fought the urge to seek out the woman's eyes again. It wasn't worth it. He knew that much from experience.

"You all right?"

Lyons tensed as an arm wrapped around his shoulder.

Schwarz had hustled to catch up with him as they left the arrests and all the associated paperwork to the Border Patrol.

"Yeah... yeah, I'm okay."

"Saw the way you were looking at that pretty *señorita*," Gadgets taunted. "She ain't Mexican, you know."

"Yeah, I know."

"Guatemalan, or Honduran maybe."

"Salvadoran."

"Oh." Schwarz's eyebrows came together. "Bona fide war zone material."

Lyons climbed into the nearest Jeep and turned up the volume on the government-band radio. "Just forget it, okay? Besides, it sounds like our job's not over." Lyons turned up the volume. Someone, somewhere, was calling for help.

Schwarz motioned toward the *banditos* sitting in the dust. "Sure, it's over. We just scored a home run tonight."

"Our job's not over," Ironman repeated as he started the Jeep. He turned up the volume, finally catching his partner's attention.

Rosario Blancanales was calling for assistance.

2

It wasn't terrorist sappers who'd climbed up along the rim of Canine Canyon toward Rosario Blancanales's position, but a haggard group of pollos, much like the family Lyons and Schwarz encountered less than a mile away. Except that one old man in the group carried a ten-foot-long flagpole, not a rocket launcher as the Able Team commando had first feared.

It was more a banner than a flagpole, actually, the man's daughter explained after the team of Border Patrol agents surrounded the group. "He is old, senile," she whispered guardedly. "He was in the Mexican army many years. He was a hero to the people of our village. This flag—the flag of his unit—it flies on our land, always. He wants to take it to America now...to fly it over his new home."

"You're kidding, of course," one of the newer border patrolmen replied with mild sarcasm.

"She's not," Patterson said, nodding his head in resignation. "This is the fifth or sixth time we've caught him coming through with his goddamn flagpole. We usually just process them, run 'em through the paperwork mill, then bus 'em back into Chihuahua."

"You're shittin' me."

"I wish I was."

"Fifth or sixth time?" the rookie questioned, scratching the stubble on his chin. "Hell, we're talking felony violation here, Chief—if you wanted to pursue it."

The supervisor frowned at that suggestion. "More paperwork than it's worth," he muttered, turning to start back to the van.

By now Blancanales had finally allowed himself to relax. He wondered if night duty was really making him that paranoid, or had the damn flagpole actually *looked* like an RPG-7 for a moment? Were the circumstances not so sad, he might have laughed.

"So what do we do with 'em?" the rookie border agent asked, holding up his hands, a bewildered expression creasing his features. "Book 'em or run 'em back through the fence or *what*?"

Patterson paused beside the van. He seemed to be contemplating the rookie's question. Blancanales watched his eyes dart down the road, and realized he wasn't pondering their present circumstances at all, but listening to the sound of an approaching engine.

Two engines, maybe three. A couple of miles down the road, approaching fast, pistons roaring. And a whine. A wail in the night.

Blancanales recognized the sound as the weak, woefully inept siren of a Border Patrol Jeep. It was the old fire engine type, but with only half the decibel noise behind it.

Politician dropped into a crouch as headlight beams appeared at a bend in the dirt road and gunshots erupted.

Patterson had turned up the van's radio and started the vehicle's engine. Blancanales monitored something about the approaching high-speed pursuit involving suspected *pollo* smugglers.

"We now have *shots fired!*" the Jeep driver was advising El Paso HQ over the radio.

"No shit!" the nearby rookie said, now ignoring the illegal aliens being detained. Blancanales followed him and the other agents as they piled into the van. Patterson swung it around, trying to block the narrow roadway.

An old blue '68 Chevrolet Super Sport swerved to the left, avoiding the cliff's vertical drop on the right as it climbed the steep hillside, plowing through mesquite and cacti, attempting to go around Patterson's van. Blancanales could see that nearly a dozen wide-eyed Hispanics were crowded into the dented two-door sedan, which bore taped-over Mexican license plates.

Why would there be shooting over just a simple illegal border crossing? he wondered as two Border Patrol Jeeps followed the Chevy around the makeshift roadblock. At that moment the van's rear tires began spinning as Patterson floored the gas pedal.

"They've got to be smuggling more than *pollos* across the line!" the senior agent commented as if reading Blancanales's mind. He then leaned into the steering wheel, and the van fishtailed, overcorrected, slid around to the other side and finally straightened out as its engine strained to propel it after the other vehicles.

The chase proceeded up the steep, winding roadway until they crested the hilltop and roared down into the valley, crossing a point where Stanton and Lerdo Streets merged in bridge fashion over the Rio Grande. The twinkling lights of El Paso suddenly appeared below, stretching like spangles on black velvet clear to the elusive line of a northeastern horizon.

The speed of all four vehicles increased dramatically now that they were racing downhill, and Blancanales could see that the Chevy's rear window had been blown out by pistol shots from the pursuing patrolmen.

Up ahead, behind the shards of shattered glass, two flashes erupted. Then the discharges reached Pol's ears: twin smacks as double-0 buckshot struck the lead Border Patrol Jeep.

"The bastards have a sawed-off!" Patterson yelled as he swung the sluggish van's steering wheel from side to side to avoid any of the pellets flying toward them.

The brunt of the blast had been absorbed by the lead Jeep's windshield and front bumper, however. Out a side window, Blancanales watched the four-wheel-drive vehicle veer off the roadway and down into a ditch, where it overturned.

"Keep on their butts!" Patterson yelled into the radio mike held to his lips by one hand while the other fought the protesting steering wheel as the remaining three vehicles flew into a sharp curve.

The second Border Patrol Jeep's brake lights had flashed on briefly—the driver obviously contemplating ending his pursuit in order to check on his buddies.

"Stay on 'em!" Patterson repeated even as the second Jeep resumed a sudden acceleration that saw pebbles and gravel thrown onto the van's windshield as its rear tires began spinning again. Without waiting for a verbal reply from the Jeep's driver, Patterson reached down, switched channels and requested additional units from El Paso to check on the overturned vehicle.

"They're already en route, Paso Two," a female dispatcher droned without emotion.

Blancanales glanced back, expecting to see the overturned Jeep burst into a fireball, but there was only the slight hint of a silver smoke column billowing up from under the hood. He watched the two border patrolmen scurry out through the crumpled passenger's side door, apparently not seriously injured.

The sight was surrealistic and sent a shiver down his spine while bringing back Carl Lyons's words, as well, something all cops were taught from day one at the academy: never stop. Hard as it might be—and despite all the mental trauma it might cause later, after the injured man died because he was abandoned on the side of the roadway with a bullet in his belly or a knife through his heart—the policy was to continue the chase. Backup units would arrive to check on the fallen cop. Your first priority as the initial chase car was to keep the suspect in sight—and appre-hend, if possible. It just wouldn't wash with the brass, *or* the Brotherhood of the Badge, to have the killer or killers get away and live to strike down some other poor, unsus-pecting cop another day.

If he were going by the book, Patterson might have pulled over to check on the men in the overturned Jeep. As it was, Blancanales surmised the Border Patrol supervisor was contemplating exactly such a move when he happened to glance in a side mirror and spot the two agents crawling out from under the smoking debris, none the worse for wear. Besides, tonight his first priority was covering the lead chase unit, the Jeep that had taken over the pursuit, in this case.

Blancanales noted that Patterson never bothered acti-vating the van's overhead emergency lights or siren. The Border Patrol Jeep speeding fifty feet ahead of them had one of the ancient, nonelectronic sirens blaring atop its left front fender well and a pitifully inadequate *Kojak* light flashing on the dashboard, but there didn't seem to be any need for much more out here in what Pol perceived to be the middle of nowhere.

Or the edge of nowhere, as the city lights grew closer, taking on individualistic sparkles as the first sign of street beacons threw a pinkish glow through the blue mist up ahead.

Their van's bouncing chassis was suddenly racing along smoothly and Blancanales realized they'd left the canyon's dirt roads behind and were now gliding along a paved ac-cess road leading toward the first of the truck toll barriers and Immigration checkpoints up ahead.

In the distance a sea of blue and red flashing lights grew rapidly larger: the El Paso office already had a V-shaped roadblock set up.

Blancanales was familiar with such felony-stop tactics: the V was pointed toward them, making it more difficult for the suspects to crash through even if they risked a high-speed impact. The problem facing the border patrolmen was twofold: first, there weren't enough INS vehicles down at the bottom of the hill to prevent their suspect from simply going around the wheeled barrier, and second, the driver of the Chevy Super Sport was obviously a madman with more than a few defensive driving tactics up his sleeve.

Blancanales glanced at the van's speedometer and saw they were doing ninety-five miles per hour. They had already overtaken the slower jeep, which was foreign-made. It had quickly topped out at about seventy-five as the three vehicles roared downhill toward the panorama of twinkling blue and yellow lights.

Blancanales shook his head. Up ahead he could already discern the outlines of several border patrolmen, their campaign hats cocked at jaunty angles, leaning over truck and Jeep hoods, their shoulders snug against shotgun stocks as they placed their weight and security against engine blocks that could stop most bullets but maybe not an entire Chevy Super Sport barreling along in excess of a hundred miles an hour.

True to fate's design—and Blancanales's intuition—the Super Sport swerved first to the right, then immediately to the left, and roared around the roadblock as if it had only been a minor inconvenience.

"Hold on to your balls!" Patterson announced as he sought to follow the suspect vehicle's course, even as agents at the roadblock unleashed a flurry of shotgun blasts at the Chevrolet's right-side wheels.

The buckshot missed, but the driver lost control of the vehicle as it raced down into the grassy ditch that dipped ten or eleven feet below the level platform of asphalt and gratings on which the checkpoint stood.

Patterson began braking a good fifty yards before reaching the roadblock, but there was nothing to suggest that he was planning to stop. The Chevy's rear wheels were still spinning violently as the car spun around and around, making soggy brown doughnuts in the wet grass as it sought dry earth and enough friction to propel it back onto the roadway.

The Border Patrol supervisor reached toward the dashboard and flicked on the flashing roof lights, hoping to avoid adding any confusion to the shotgun-toting troopers' already bizarre working conditions. He gunned the accelerator, and tried to race around on the right to cut off the Chevy, but suddenly a slender Mexican with a bold Zapata mustache leaned out the SS's passenger side window and blasted away with a Mossberg 12-gauge.

The van's windshield shattered as buckshot slammed into it, causing a spiderweb of silver slashes. Pieces of the safety glass proved not so safe after all as they hit Patterson and the agent riding next to him with full force in the face and chest.

Both men leaned back in their seats as if struck with sledgehammers. Patterson brought his forearms up over his face in something akin to a blood-smeared crucifix. The other agent let out an unearthly scream as he fought to hold his lower jaw in place; it had nearly been torn away by the double-barreled blast.

"Shit!" Blancanales yelled as he rushed up between the two rookies crowding the front section of the van's passenger compartment and climbed over the vehicle's gearshift and transmission assembly box.

"You okay, Patterson?"

Without waiting for a reply, the Able Team commando pulled the big man out from behind the steering wheel and slid into his seat as the van headed straight for an open trench behind the checkpoints.

"I'm...I'm all right!" Patterson said, wiping blood and sweat from his eyes and forehead. "Just got some shit in my face, man! Can you take over till I get my act together?'' He was already turning to assist the other injured agent.

Blancanales's actions spoke for him as he jerked the steering wheel to the left and guided the van back up onto the pavement. Momentarily he bent low to his right, and reached for the microphone, which had fallen onto the floorboards. Relief surged through him as he realized the device hadn't been damaged. "This is Patterson's unit!" the Able Team commando spoke into the mike, unsure of the proper radio call signs yet forcing a calm demeanor that wasn't quite reflected in his face. "Requesting assistance. In pursuit on the main drag running north-south into El Paso from the INS checkpoint above Canine Canyon!" Not quite familiar enough with the area's official topographical designations, either, he threw in every landmark he could think of. "I have two wounded agents on board. I need backup, *now*!"

"Unit transmitting," came the same steady female voice over the radio network, "please *identify*!" Her tone told Blancanales she didn't quite believe his current situation but that she sure as hell wanted to know who had commandeered a Border Patrol transmitter!

"Give me that!" Patterson ordered, reaching for the mike. Blancanales quickly handed it to him, glad to have both hands on the steering wheel. But before the senior border patrolman could lend some semblance of official authority to the radio exchange, one of the agents back at the roadblock began tying up the network.

"El Paso, this is Checkpoint Paisano. That was Paso Two, Agent Patterson's unit. He's now headed northbound Stanton toward Highway 62. We'll be right on his tail shortly. See if you can get some units headed south from downtown."

"And have paramedics on standby!" another voice advised the people in Communications. "We've got wounded everywhere!"

"Roger your last, Paso Six!" A bit of excitement now laced the dispatcher's voice.

As he held on to the steering wheel and practically stood on the gas pedal, stomping it into the floorboards, Blancanales envisioned the woman finally setting aside her Joseph Wambaugh novel and devoting all of her attention to the men racing about in the field.

"Fire Dispatch has already got an ambulance and pumper headed for Paso Three's Ten-Twenty," the Border Patrol dispatcher informed everybody.

"Paso Three to Dispatch!" a new voice came over the air. Blancanales knew it was the driver of the Jeep that had overturned back on the canyon trail. "No injuries at this location. I repeat, no injuries. Cancel paramedics but keep the pumper rolling. Our unit's totally engulfed in flames!"

"Ten-four, Paso Three. Advising Fire Dispatch at this time."

"Turn that ambulance around!" Patterson yelled into his mike as two bars of flashing light raced toward them head-on, and a station wagon and fire truck roared past, speeding in the opposite direction, en route to Paso Three's crash site. "I want the EMTs right behind us when we catch up to this slime." He winked at Blancanales, forefinger off the microphone's transmit lever now as his other hand kept a pressure bandage against the wounded agent's jaw. "'Cause those lowlifes in the Chevy are gonna *need* it!"

"Never seen no wetbacks put this much effort into gettin' away!" one of the rookies in the back of the van commented as he struggled to make his way back toward Patterson's blood-smeared headrest.

"That's cause you've got less days on this job than I've got dimples on my ass, kid!" Patterson responded.

"You okay?" Blancanales glanced over at the senior agent as the van's engine strained to catch up with the souped-up Chevrolet.

"I'll be all right," Patterson answered, waving Rosario's look of concern off as he used the other hand to swab at rivulets of blood streaking his forehead. "Just a couple of scalp wounds from the flying glass. Looks worse than it is—scalp wounds bleed a lot, you know."

"I know," Blancanales said, gritting his teeth.

"Hurts like hell, though," Patterson admitted.

"What about your partner?"

"He'll be fine if this chase doesn't last all night and we can get him a Medevac."

"I'll see what I can do," Blancanales returned, stomping on the gas pedal.

The Chevy SS had suddenly slowed as if it had run out of gas or into mechanical trouble, and Patterson drew his side arm for the first time. Lowering the wounded patrolman against the gearbox, he leaned halfway out the van's passenger side window and aimed the long-barreled Smith & Wesson Model 28 at the Super Sport's rear trunk.

Dual puffs of black smoke from the car's exhaust pipes made him hesitate, however. And then the sound reached them: the SS's driver had floored the engine into overdrive. Simultaneously his accomplice wielding the shotgun fired another volley of double-0 buck back at their pursuers. The .25-caliber pellets slammed into the Border Patrol van's front grill but inflicted no immediately apparent damage on the engine.

"Them south-o'-the-border bastards!" Patterson yelled. Extending only his forearm and gun hand this time, he popped off six rounds at the Chevrolet as it began pulling away again.

The men in the Border Patrol van heard a single impact up ahead—only one of Patterson's shots had hit the target. Not bad for a "rolling gun battle," as they'd call it back at the police academy. Blancanales recalled another of Lyons's old LAPD stories: every self-professed expert at the pistol range claimed that ninety-nine percent of the bullets fired at or from a speeding vehicle skipped down the road without hitting the target. One out of ten caused damage to private property somewhere along the way: parked cars or house windows or storefronts. Another one out of a hundred actually struck a pedestrian or someone inside a dwelling unlucky enough to be in the wrong place at the wrong time. In other words, firing from or at a speeding vehicle just wasn't worth it.

That was the official line, anyway.

Carl Lyons had a different opinion, as usual. He believed that ricocheting hot lead off the pavement immediately behind the pursued car would—fifty percent of the time—see the bullets bounce eight or nine inches off the asphalt and into the vehicle's undercarriage, often damaging the gas tank or rear wheels. Usually.

"Try placing your next six rounds right into the blacktop behind that mother's rear taillights!" Blancanales suggested, watching out of the corner of one eye as Patterson brought out two speed strips.

"You're probably just like my son-in-law," Patterson complained as he wasted time with the old-fashioned rubber speed strip. "He's always tryin' to get me to switch over to... what do you call 'em? *Fastloaders*."

"Speedloaders."

"Uh, right."

Blancanales glanced down at the van's dashboard. Every light was flashing red: Overheat, Oil, Transmission Fluid, Brakes. But the vehicle continued to race along with no loss of power, and that was all that mattered to Politician.

"Well, here goes," Patterson declared, slamming the Model 28's cylinder shut. "Got nothing much to lose!"

Leaning out the window so that he could get a decent sighting, he took Blancanales's advice. Slowly, gently, he squeezed off all six rounds before dropping back into his seat again.

The Chevy's right rear tire exploded, and sparks billowed out along the outside of the car like a Fourth of July fireworks fountain. Within seconds the tire's rubber shreds flapped themselves to the point of disintegration, but the Super Sport continued speeding down the road, its right rear wheel listing noticeably on a battered rim.

"Try another six!" Blancanales yelled. "Didn't see it before, but I notice you pull to the right when you shoot—"

"Well, excuse the shit out of me," Patterson said, cutting him off as he reached for another speed strip.

"No offense," Blancanales returned, ignoring the retort as the speed of the pursuit dropped to a manageable level. "But aim slightly left of the chassis this time. See if you can knock out the other tire!"

"I don't think even *that's* gonna stop this bastard!" Patterson answered, noting that both vehicles were still racing along at seventy to seventy-five miles per hour. "But you got it, brother!"

Blancanales glanced at the rearview mirror. The Border Patrol units from the checkpoint were trying to catch up to the chase; he counted nearly a half-dozen separate vehicles a half mile or so back. But at these speeds he didn't think they'd be of any use until the pursuit ended.

Their extra guns would come in handy then, because he was certain that these coyotes weren't going down without a fight.

"We got company!" one of the agents in the back of the van called out. He sounded relieved.

Blancanales glanced to his left. On a major roadway several hundred feet to the west, running parallel to their chase, another Border Patrol Jeep was racing along at an extremely fast clip—actually outspeeding the chase itself. But the new Jeep seemed too far away to do Blancanales, Patterson or his people any good.

"That's Juárez Street over there," the senior Border Patrol agent said, squinting in the direction of the distant INS Jeep. On its roof was a display of flashing red, white and blue lights—in fact, more emergency equipment was mounted on top of the vehicle than all the other Border Patrol units combined. "And that looks like Cooper's Renegade!" Patterson added, an impish grin contorting his previously somber features. "He's got a goddamn V-8 under the hood—installed the sucker himself!"

"Maybe he plans on cutting the bad guys off at the pass," Pol remarked sarcastically, little hope in his expression.

Patterson's tone was a rebuking one. "If anyone can, Cooper can," he said with certainty. The Renegade was swerving in and out of slower-moving traffic like a jackrabbit hopping between a group of beached turtles. "Never seen him drive so recklessly before, though."

"An agent's been shot," one of the rookies in the back of the van said, as if in explanation.

Patterson didn't need a reminder. "*Three* agents have been wounded!" he said grimly. "Three I know of."

"We can sure use the heat he's packin' tonight!" the rookie in the rear of the van told them. "I saw Cooper checkin' out an armful of CAR-15s from the armory before we hit the road after roll call!"

Blancanales matched Patterson's nod. They *could* use the firepower once the chase was over. He didn't like the idea of going up against a sawed-off shotgun with mere revolvers, regardless of the circumstances.

What he didn't realize was that Carl "Ironman" Lyons was behind the steering wheel of Agent Cooper's souped-up Renegade.

3

The Renegade was waiting at the top of the overpass when Blancanales's high-speed chase passed the L375 freeway loop and turned onto the multilaned Highway 62, heading into the heart of El Paso.

As if bored by all the sirens and flashing lights, Lyons calmly pulled up beside Blancanales as the two Border Patrol vehicles barreled toward the maze of ramps that could take them deeper into the heart of El Paso along Highway 54, or perhaps southeast on Interstate 10, back down along the border.

Blancanales grabbed the mike from Patterson. As if by reflex, the senior agent reached down and switched the radio frequency to a car-to-car channel. "Well, what are you waiting for?" Pol yelled into the microphone as he stared out the driver's side window, locking eyes with Ironman, who responded with an evil death's-head grin. "Go get them!"

Raising both elbows nonchalantly as his shoulders dipped in a calm shrug, Lyons nodded and floored the Renegade's gas pedal.

The agents in Blancanales's van watched the powerful Jeep, occupied by at least five additional peace officers in the front and back seats, surge forward with a sudden thrust.

The Border Patrol van was left behind in the resulting plumes of exhaust smoke and fumes, and Lyons's vehicle rapidly halved the distance between its front bumper and the Chevy Super Sport's tail pipes.

Before reaching the freeway, Patterson had fired off another cylinder and one of the bullets had struck pay dirt—the *left* tire this time. However, this development only seemed to serve the coyotes' long range goals; now both rear wheels were riding on rims. The rear end of the chassis had leveled out, allowing the vehicle to go faster, and now sparks shot out from *both* sides of the Chevy's underbelly, too. But everyone was aware the fiasco couldn't last much longer, since the rims would eventually melt down or warp.

"Maybe Ironman can punch some holes in the sucker's gas tank," Blancanales mused as he struggled to keep up with the chase. "Those sparks would turn that Super Sport into a rolling inferno!"

"We should *be* so lucky," Patterson said. The supervisor didn't sound optimistic. After a pause, during which screeching sirens and protesting pistons from a half-dozen vehicles filled their ears, he added, "Actually I'd kind of like to capture them alive! Ask 'em some questions, then book 'em on charges of attempted murder of a federal agent." He glanced over at the wounded patrolman.

The man was slipping into shock. Patterson applied a fresh bandage in a vain attempt to hold the nearly severed lower jaw immobile as the van rocked and rolled down the roadway.

"I hear where you're coming from!" Blancanales gritted his teeth as the pursuit continued northbound onto Highway 54 toward the Fort Bliss military post. "Don't you think *I'd* like to get my hands on the scum, too? Find out what they're smuggling aboard that crate that's so important they'd risk popping caps on cops to get it across the border?"

"Then let's do it!" Patterson leaned forward in his seat and stretched his arms out. "I'm gettin' tired of the ride, *Rosario*. And I've seen Fort Bliss before."

"Shit!" Blancanales jerked the steering wheel hard to the right as the Chevy and Lyons's Renegade suddenly veered toward an off ramp. He barely made the exit, and the van started to fishtail to the left, but he corrected in time. In his peripheral vision a highway sign's reflectorized letters proclaimed, Pershing Drive. "Where does this take us?" he asked Patterson as they sped down the off ramp toward red signal lights at the bottom of a sloping hill.

"If he veers east—to the right—we'll be smack-dab inside the west gate of Fort Bliss. If he turns left, we'll head back into the heart of downtown El Paso toward Magoffin Home."

"Magoffin *what*?"

"It's a historical point of interest, which means trouble for us, because there's a favorite park nearby that the teenyboppers like to frequent—even this late at night. I hate to think of this dude broadsiding a hot rod packed with double-daters."

"Any luck the MPs at Bliss will be able to assist?"

"Looks like they're already moving into position!" Patterson said, pointing at four olive drab Malibus assembling at the bottom of the ramp, their roof lights flashing.

A huge, phantomlike shape dropping from above caught Blancanales's attention as he approached the fort. Like a beast emerging from the belly of the storm clouds drifting overhead, the eerie shape suddenly became recognizable as it pierced the low-lying fog bank. A blue strobe mounted beneath the fuselage identified the craft as a Singapore Airlines jumbo jet. "They allow 747s to land at Bliss?" Blancanales asked, sounding intrigued despite the circumstances.

Suspecting that this mysterious, Pentagon-dispatched commando wouldn't mention the Boeing unless it could somehow be used to benefit their current circumstances. Patterson quickly replied, "It ain't landing at Bliss. El Paso International Airport's located on the other side of the Army post."

"Oh." Blancanales's jaw was firmly set now. "Guess it don't matter much, no how...eh, Patterson?"

The coyote piloting the souped-up Chevy had turned left, away from the military post. A shower of sparks from the Super Sport's rear end settled over the disappointed MPs, who would now be unable to participate in the chase because the vehicle had failed to enter their post, even briefly.

Out of the corner of his eye, Blancanales noticed one of the military policemen slamming the hood of his patrol car after reholstering his .45 pistol, his clean-shaven face lined with youthful disappointment.

As he brought the van skidding down across the three westbound lanes of Pershing Drive, Blancanales couldn't purge the image of the MP's face from his mind. Nineteen. The kid couldn't have been more than nineteen—full of energy and youthful ambition, eager to tackle Lady Death in his quest for danger and excitement. At that age they all considered themselves immortal. Had it really been that long since Rosario himself was such a tender age?

And to think that he could even be worrying about lost years while his bone-white knuckles fought to keep from losing control of the Border Patrol van.

"Earth to Pol," Blancanales muttered to himself as the chase proceeded deeper into the heart of the city.

"What?" Patterson asked, reaching for the mike dangling from the dashboard as the Able Team warrior brought the van to within twenty feet of Lyons's rear bumper.

"Nothing!" Blancanales shot back, a smile growing involuntarily—all memory of the teenage MP gone, images of the approaching firefight filling his head instead.

"Proceeding southwest along Pershing Drive," Patterson advised the dispatchers in Communication, only a few scant miles away now.

There was very little traffic on the wide boulevard. Taxis sat alongside the road here and there, their parking lights glowing faintly. Darkened storefronts pressed against windswept sidewalks. Four- and five-story apartment buildings rose behind the closed businesses, most of their windows black, as well. Streetlights flashed by like matchsticks tossed from a speeding train into the uncaring night.

"Tell me this racetrack dead-ends somewhere," Blananales groaned as they roared down into an older section of the city where homeless bums slept on bus benches, and painted ladies of questionable virtue haunted dimly lit doorways even at this late hour.

"Up ahead we encounter a real mess," Patterson said in the emotionless monotone of a bored tour guide. "That's Throwbridge Drive coming up on your left there, then ... *watch out!*"

At Throwbridge four of El Paso's finest were waiting. Boasting two late-model Caprices, a Chrysler Le Baron and a Plymouth Fury with a police package under the hood, the two-tone units, which appeared dull bronze under the streetlights' artificial illumination, charged out in front of the Super Sport, attempting to run it off the T-intersection and into a parking lot.

The grinning coyote swerved hard to his left, crashed up into the parking lot's perimeter of hip-high anchor chain and rode the sagging barrier for a half block before slamming back down onto blacktop and continuing southwest along Pershing Drive.

"And up ahead we have Montana and Copia Streets," Patterson continued, the ever-present, jaded comedian. "I wager he'll bypass both and continue southwest along Pershing. The Mexicans *love* to beat feet along Pershing."

Glancing over his shoulder, he shook his head at the plight of the El Paso police cars, which had all skidded to the side of the road to let Lyons, then Blancanales and finally two additional Border Patrol units whip by.

"You've been in a chase down this avenue before?" Blancanales asked incredulously.

"Sure," Patterson said. "Just never escalated into a goddamn shooting war like this before," he added as he reloaded his revolver.

Just as the senior Border Patrol agent had predicted, the Super Sport continued along Pershing Drive.

"This is going to go on forever," complained one of the patrolmen in the back seat. He was nursing bumps and bruises from repeatedly slamming his head against the van's roof each time they crashed through a dip in the roadway.

"Not for *us* it ain't," Blancanales said, pointing at the fuel gauge. "We're flying on fumes, *amigo*!"

Apparently Lyons was too, Blancanales thought as he watched his colleague's vehicle. Or else he was running out of patience with the crazy coyote behind the Chevy's steering wheel. Without warning Ironman began gunning the Renegade. It surged forward and rammed the Super Sport's rear bumper once, twice, three times.

The Chevy swerved wildly to the left, crossing the oncoming lanes, then back to the right, overcorrecting as it sideswiped a parked car, sending an even higher wall of sparks showering down on the pursuing units.

"He's *headed* somewhere," Blancanales said, biting into his lower lip.

"No shit," yelled one of the patrolmen in the back seat as he clutched the back of Pol's headrest. "He's headed to hell with us right behind!"

"I don't mean *that*!" Blancanales shook off the lapse in mental concentration. "He's trying to get somewhere. The punk's heading home. Maybe he has help waiting for him there, or something.... I don't know."

"Anyone tries to help that hairball gets his balls busted, too!" someone said.

"Hell, his home's back down in Mexico, man!" the first patrolman muttered.

"Let's just say I've got a feeling on this one!" the Able Team expert predicted as he cast caution to the wind and stomped on the gas pedal one last time, ignoring the fuel gauge as, up ahead, Lyons rammed the Super Sport from behind again.

In the distance the tall twin spires of a brick church loomed suddenly out from the darkness—a bastion of tradition and security against the impending uncertainty of law and order, crime and punishment, cops and robbers racing toward it at high speed.

Blancanales's Border Patrol van sputtered, and Lyons rammed the Chevy one last time, gunning the Renegade's engine as he did so.

Rear rims smoldering, the Super Sport's back axle fractured from the impact, and the sedan fishtailed to the left. Its front end rose into the air, and the entire car flipped over onto its side, struck an illegally parked Volvo and burst into flames. It crashed down through a padlocked vendor's newspaper rack and came to rest on its roof at the front steps of the church, spinning slowly counterclockwise.

Lyons pulled his vehicle up on the left, Blancanales on the right. Both men had killed their sirens, although the irritating noise still came from many of the police cars pulling up behind them as excited officers piled out of their vehicles with service revolvers drawn, neglecting to shut down the emergency equipment. Some brandished shotguns. Red and blue shards of hot light splashed across the dull gray brick of Saint Michael's Church, whose twin spires pierced the night sky.

Screams filled the evening air. Men were burning alive inside the glowing Chevy two-door as its driver and one other man scampered out through the shattered side window and sprinted up the long line of stairs into the church.

By the time the El Paso Fire Department's jaws-of-life squad arrived on the scene ten minutes later, Supervisor Robert Patterson had determined that eight illegal aliens had been squeezed into the cramped quarters of the two-door sedan. Six of those had perished.

The driver and his accomplice had managed to make their way through the church's massive front oak doors in all the confusion.

Sanctuary, the age-old savior, immortalized by many a Hollywood tearjerker. Make it to the church and to its sympathetic parishioners and priest and you were home free.

Well, not in Rosario Blancanales's book. That kind of crap happened in the movies and nowhere else. Politician wasn't about to humor the scum. This was the big time, boys—hot pursuit. He hoped Patterson would see it that way, too.

Blancanales wasted no time waiting for someone to issue orders. Though he felt it out-of-bounds to enter the church first, on his own, the commando quickly issued directives for the nearest group of border patrolmen to surround the sprawling church and its wrought-iron-enclosed grounds. In the background someone called in a hospital helicopter to airlift the critically wounded agent in Patterson's van.

Within another ten minutes the El Paso PD had nearly forty officers supplementing Patterson's ranks.

"Fancy meeting you dudes here," Pol commented, reaching out and slapping Gadgets on the back as the three men of Able Team rushed up the four or five dozen concrete stairs leading to the church's front entrance. Behind them, the flight-for-life chopper was already flaring in for a middle-of-the-intersection landing—it had been hovering above the chase soon after the Officer Down calls first went out over the airwaves.

"It's our pleasure," Lyons said, winking. "You never *could* keep a high-speed pursuit down to under a ten-block radius, Pol."

"You were just itching to get in on it, and you know it," Blancanales returned, smiling as Schwarz tossed him a CAR-15. He glanced up at the thick wooden doors separating them from their two suspects—the doors must have been a good thirty feet high. "Feels kind of creepy carrying these things into a church," he said, holding up the assault rifle.

"They chose to end it on the altar," Lyons answered, not sounding as reverent. "We're here to oblige them."

On the steps below, a patrol commander from the El Paso PD was confronting Supervisor Patterson but yielding to his unspoken status as top cop on the scene, since the Border Patrol had initiated the chase.

"What's your game plan?" the silver-haired police captain asked as he glanced up at the Able Team trio, suspicion lacing his tense features.

Patterson turned toward a border patrolman standing midway down the sidewalk corridor that led behind the church. "Has the perimeter been secured yet?" he called out.

"All secure!" the agent shouted back with a thumbs-up for emphasis.

"I guess we go in!" Patterson said, locking eyes with Blancanales as he spoke to the captain.

"Uh," the captain began, "don't you think we should have one of my people make land line contact with the priests inside and let them know what's going on, maybe have them meet us at the front door?"

"What do you say, Rosario?" Patterson asked, rushing up the thirty-odd steps and reaching Blancanales's side without breaking a sweat.

"We're in hot pursuit of felony shooters," Lyons cut in. "I don't need permission from any priest to enter a—"

"What's going on here?" One of the big front doors had burst open without warning, and over a dozen law officers wearing the uniforms of three or four different agencies dropped into defensive crouches, gun arms extended toward the Catholic church's facade, hammers cocked as a man, clad in a black suit and white clerical collar, emerged.

The priest didn't fit Lyons's preconceived image. He was in his early thirties, had a full head of thick black hair and carried the posture-perfect physique of a body builder. "What *is* the meaning of this?" the priest asked, more insistent this time. "I heard footsteps. I was awakened by the sound of running, but there was no one outside the rectory. I thought I was dreaming, then I heard all the sirens outside."

Blancanales detected a faint Spanish accent, though the priest's features seemed only vaguely Hispanic. "We were chasing some *pollo* smugglers, Father."

"My *God*!" The priest's eyes darted past Blancanales and down the long line of concrete steps leading away from the church's doors. He took in the carnage in the parking lot below: ambulances were forming a cordon, in the style of a wagon train, around several corpses lying on the blacktop beneath bright yellow and orange fire department blankets. The smoldering upside down Super Sport sat in the middle of all the activity like a pagan idol at a headhunter's sacrificial ceremony. "I must attend to them..." He started to rush down the steps, only to be stopped by Patterson's viselike grip on his wrist.

"The suspects, my friend..." Patterson's chin rose to show who was in charge, who granted permission for *anyone* to move from this point onward.

"I am Father Felipe," the priest said, his eyes wide but clouded with fatigue. He followed Patterson's motion toward the cavern of darkness inside the church. Blancanales was relieved to see that there was no midnight mass taking place inside.

"We need to go inside," Patterson said, his eyes drilling into the priest's now, trying to hypnotize the clergyman, place him under the spell of authority.

"We chased them all the way from the border," Blancanales whispered into the priest's ear. "They fired on us. Several of our people were injured." He gestured toward the fire-engine-red Huey slowly ascending above the frantic swirl of activity in the parking lot and street below. "They crashed the car and left the innocent *pollos* they'd held captive inside the Chevy to burn in a ball of flames." The words left his lips almost mechanically as he worked at the will of the exhausted priest.

"Yes... yes, of course," Father Felipe said, nodding as he watched the flight-for-life chopper's nose dip slightly before its pilot pulled pitch and the craft roared off over the dangerous jungle of telephone and power lines. "Do what you must do. Men fleeing murder will find no sanctuary at Saint Michael's. Now I must tend to those who have perished." He broke free of Patterson's grasp and started down the steps again.

"Let's go!" Lyons shouted, the barrel of his CAR-15 raised skyward. "I'll take the lead and—"

"You'll do no such thing!"

The men clustered around Blancanales and Patterson froze as the second door flew open and two more figures crowded the entryway. These priests were older—in their early sixties or so—with less hair and more weight riding their waistlines. Like Father Felipe, they were dressed in black with white collars. They also appeared to be of Spanish or Italian descent.

"I am Father Franco," one of the priests announced, knocking Lyons's rifle barrel down. "And just *who* are you people?" he demanded. His eyes did a once-over of all three Able Team commandos, taking in their ragged clothes and disheveled appearance.

"We're, uh . . ." Blancanales hesitated, aware that the priest probably wouldn't believe anything he had to say.

"We're with the police," Lyons answered in a courteous but firm tone. "And we haven't got time to dick around outside here, Father, with all due respect."

Father Franco's eyes shot past Ironman, locking onto Patterson's.

"They're with a Pentagon think tank," the border patrol agent confirmed, smiling thinly, "based in Washington, D.C."

Father Franco surveyed Lyons's features. "You must be joking!" he exclaimed finally.

"Not hardly." Lyons was fast losing patience. He started to brush past the two priests, then hesitated, glancing back at Patterson.

"Now *I* think you'd best cooperate," one of the young border patrolmen accompanying Patterson suggested as he moved forward. He had been a good friend of the injured agent and was in no mood for niceties.

"Back off, Anderson," Patterson ordered.

"You're in charge," Blancanales interjected as he stared at the senior border patrolman. "Give us the go-ahead."

Patterson was determined not to appear intimidated by representatives of what some might construe to be a supreme authority. "Give it your best shot," he told Lyons, ignoring Father Franco now. "Just try not to shoot up any stained glass windows, okay?"

"I protest! You can't do *this*!" Father Franco exploded. He and the priest standing beside him both threw up their hands in horror. "This is sacrilege! It's a travesty! Do you hear me? It's a travesty!"

"No one is above the law, Father," Patterson said, "not even you priests or your *pollos*, and like the man here al-

ready told you—'' he motioned toward Carl Lyons—
''we're in hot pursuit.''

''God's commandments transcend man's laws,'' Father
Franco shot back.

''Well, sir, I don't know of any commandment that pro-
hibits me from arresting felons or entering a house of worship to do it. Now if you'll excuse us.''

''You cannot enter Saint Michael's carrying those weapons!'' Franco's fellow clergyman warned.

''The coyotes are in there, Father,'' Patterson said. He
wasn't a religious man, and had no idea how to address the
two, but was hoping to minimize the complaints that would
surely result after tonight. ''I'm sure *they're* armed. I'm not
about to send these men after them without the necessary
weapons to defend themselves.'' He motioned toward the
bustle of activity at the foot of the steps. ''I suggest you
assist Father Felipe down there with—''

''You needn't address me like a child, Officer!'' Father
Franco snapped.

''Very well,'' Patterson said nodding to two border patrolmen before turning his back on the priests. The young
agents took hold of the priests' elbows and escorted them
down the steps toward the smoldering Chevy Super Sport.
''Anybody get a good look at the two wetbacks?'' he
shouted in Blancanales's direction.

Pol glanced down at Father Franco and saw all three
priests cringe at use of the term.

''One was in his late twenties,'' Schwarz answered. He
was the most observant of the group. ''Long shoulder-
length brown hair, balding at the crown, droopy mustache, boxer's nose, checkered shirt...''

''Anything else?'' Patterson asked with mild sarcasm. He
hadn't been expecting such a detailed description.

''Nope, sorry, that's it!''

''Second scum bag?''

"Early thirties, medium-length black hair, lot of gold chains around his neck, black T-shirt, tattoos on both forearms, three or four days' growth of beard."

"The T-shirt was purple," Lyons corrected.

The electronics wizard hesitated, then quickly nodded. "You're right."

"Who goes first?" the El Paso Police captain asked, standing over them now. Blancanales judged his height at somewhere around six foot six.

"I do," Lyons said lowering the business end of his rifle in preparation for entering the dark church.

"Nobody goes yet," Patterson ordered. He reached out to take a bullhorn that one of his border patrolmen had produced. "Stand back." He positioned himself against the doorframe, ensuring he had adequate cover from any outgoing projectiles, then tested the bullhorn's power switch. A deafening screech filled the entryway. "It works," he said, cocking a surprised eyebrow.

Taking a deep breath, Patterson leaned into the doorway, expecting a bullet to part his sweat-slick forehead at any moment. "This is Border Patrol Supervisor Patterson!" he shouted. The echo that rolled through the church and jumped back at them startled every man crouching in the entryway. "I'm ordering you to surrender. Exit the church with your hands in plain sight! You won't be harmed."

Patterson clicked off the bullhorn and turned to face Lyons again. "Did any of you guys see any weapons? That shotgun? The revolver?"

"I'm sure they're packing the same heat they fired during the chase," Blancanales said. "Do you want me to translate?" he asked, motioning toward the bullhorn.

"I've got it," Patterson said, frowning, and he repeated the directive to surrender in Spanish.

"They're not coming out," Schwarz observed.

"Good." Lyons jerked back the charging handle on his assault rifle and chambered a round as the four of them leaned into the dark entryway. "*Now* can I go in?"

"Wait a second," Patterson said as he visually homed in on an old woman sitting ramrod straight in a front pew on the right side of the church. She was about seventy-five yards in from the entrance. "We've got to get that old girl out of there," he said.

"She must be frozen with fear," Gadgets added, shaking his head, feeling genuine sympathy for the woman.

"Madam!" Patterson called to her, using the bullhorn again. "Stand up and come to the front entrance at once. Do you hear me? I want you to walk over here now."

But the old woman refused to budge. Blancanales squinted. Had she crossed herself? Or clutched at her breast?

"You'll hear from the church's lawyers about this!" Father Franco threatened, waving an index finger up at them in holy reprimand.

Lyons's chin lifted, but Patterson silenced the Able Team commando with a gentle palm against the chest. "Ignore him," he said, grinning tightly. "He knows not what he sayeth, son."

Patterson locked eyes with Father Franco, however. "The old woman in there!" he called down to the priest. "What's her problem? What's she doing in there this time of night?"

"The church is her home," Father Felipe replied for the tight-lipped older clergyman as he performed the last rites on a decapitated corpse lying beside the overturned Super Sport. "Her name is Martinez. She's half deaf."

"She just sits there all night?" Patterson asked.

A cynical look in his eyes, Father Felipe glanced up from the blood-soaked body at his knees. "She's not a party animal, Mr. Patterson."

"Uh, right."

"I'm out of here," Lyons announced, and he dived through the entryway and into the dark chasm that led into the vestibule.

"Watch your butt," Patterson whispered as Blancanales, then Schwarz lined up to follow him in.

4

Clouds of drifting incense—remnants of a sacred baptismal ceremony earlier that night—still shrouded the altar, fifty rows of pews away. There were no lights on inside the main worshiping area of the church, but a hundred or so small candles in red jars, off to the left, gave a crimson tint to the eerie scene.

An aisle separated the pews down the middle, ending at the raised altar. Above the altar itself, a ten-foot-high cross hung suspended from the ceiling, the tortured figure of Christ nailed to its polished wood. The porcelain face of Jesus seemed to stare sadly down at Lyons, Schwarz and Blancanales as they slowly approached the altar single file.

Faint shafts of what could only be starlight pierced the huge stained glass windows surrounding the suspended crucifix, creating an odd glow throughout the floating incense. Lyons paused behind a marble pillar before moving cautiously forward. He waved Schwarz up to his former position. Blancanales, in turn, stepped up to where Gadgets had been crouching. They would clear the entire church in this manner, if need be.

The dark wooden pews were empty except for front row center where the old woman still sat. Her back was as stiff as an ironing board. Her gray hair was done up in a bun and covered with a silk scarf in the old churchgoing tradition.

"¡Señora!" Lyons whispered harshly to her.

But still the woman didn't move. Had she been kneeling, bowed in prayer, Lyons might not have found her actions—or inaction—so strange. But just sitting there? Staring straight ahead? At least he *assumed* she was staring straight ahead. From where he was he couldn't see her face clearly, nor her eyes.

"Ironman," Schwarz hissed under his breath.

Without speaking, Lyons turned, eyes darting beyond Gadgets, well aware his name had been uttered in warning. He checked out the unmoving shadows to the left, then the right.

Nothing.

His gaze shifted back to Schwarz, and he followed his partner's hand signals, glancing to the right, a few pews beyond the old woman, near the east exit.

He could see them now—on their bellies, crawling more like frightened *pollos* attempting to slither across the border rather than cruel, bullying coyotes. But instead of moving toward the exits they were rushing straight for the old lady. And the Mexican in the lead had a sawed-off shotgun balanced across his wrists.

Lyons's eyes shifted across to the old lady again. She remained seated, frozen in terror, refusing to budge.

If bullets began to fly, she would surely be caught in the cross fire. And if the men from Stony Man Farm held off, the confrontation would deteriorate into a hostage situation—no doubt about it.

There was no time to consult a soothsayer or Ouija board over the best course of action. In any case, Lyons believed he knew the only way to react.

Making sure both Blancanales and Schwarz saw his signal, he tapped his chest with his right thumb. He then dropped his gun hand and pointed directly at the crawling Mexicans, who were now less than twenty feet from the old woman.

When Gadgets and Politician nodded their acknowledgment, Ironman wasted no more time. Filling the entire church with a chilling war cry, he jumped up onto the nearest pew and raced across nearly a dozen bench backs until he dropped down between the two coyotes.

He placed the barrel of his CAR-15 against the top of the lead crawler's skull. "Tell your buddy to drop his weapon, or they're going to need a bucketful of holy water to mop up what's left of your brains, *señor*," Lyons directed calmly, in contrast to the blood-curdling scream that had left his lips only a few seconds earlier.

The Mexican with the Mossberg trembled violently. "No shoot, *señor*!" the man pleaded. He allowed the shotgun to roll down off his wrists, and attempted to cover the top of his head with cupped hands. Back in the entryway, Patterson listened to the shotgun's dull metallic clang reverberate off the church's cavernous walls.

"Tell him," Ironman demanded.

"He...he has no gun, *señor*," the shaking coyote said, sneering at his partner. "He left it in the car!"

By then Blancanales and Schwarz had joined Lyons. The men resumed functioning as a well-drilled team, grabbing ankles and sliding the prisoners several feet away from each other before kicking limbs out to the sides and performing a cursory frisk. That finished they secured the coyotes with flexi-cuffs.

The lead coyote had been true to his word: his younger partner was unarmed.

"Hey, check this out!" Blancanales said after picking the Mossberg up off the floor. With one hand he worked the pump action repeatedly. The weapon's slide slapped smoothly three, then four times—each time revealing an empty breech.

"Out of ammo?" Lyons asked, his lower jaw dropping.

"He certainly was."

"Now the really bad news," Schwarz muttered. He had lowered his weapon and was staring over the old woman a few feet away, the fingers of his left hand probing her throat.

"Don't tell me," Lyons said, slowly closing his eyes.

"Dead as a doorknob," Gadgets told him, nodding. "Scared to death, I'd say."

"Two clichés in a row," Blancanales said, shaking his head in resignation. "But who's counting, right?"

"Cardiac arrest?" Lyons asked, his eyes narrowing as his ears detected Patterson's heavy footsteps approaching cautiously.

"Looks that way," Schwarz verified.

Carl Lyons, ex-LAPD supercop, jabbed one of the coyotes with the flash suppressor of his CAR-15. "I'd call that an unnatural death, scum bag," he said grimly. "Core Zero during the commission of a violent crime. That means you *ain't* going back south of the border with a busload of other deportees. You're going up to the Monkey House, chump—murder *one*."

"Two counts." Patterson's words sliced through the tension like a hot knife through butter as his gun hand adjusted the volume control of the walkie-talkie on his belt. "My agent, the one being airlifted by flight-for-life, was DOA at the hospital helipad. They didn't even make it to the emergency room."

Blancanales read the guilt on Patterson's features. "It couldn't have been helped," Pol said softly. "On the street we have policies...procedures. We all know the risks when we take up the gun."

"Or put on the badge," Lyons added.

"Somebody call a priest," Schwarz called over to the collection of uniforms clustered outside the front doors, an arsenal of exotic automatic weapons in their possession, ready for a PD-authorized workout. It wouldn't come tonight, at least not in El Paso.

"Two counts, not to mention the poor guys lying outside in the street," Patterson muttered to himself.

"Five bucks says the Fathers Three are tying up the phone lines right about now," Blancanales offered blandly, "trying to get through to a lawyer." After a moment of reflection, he added, "You know, too much of this kind of outrageous bullshit could drive a good Saigon commando sane."

Ironman matched his grim smile, but something told the San Ysidro native that he and Lyons weren't amused by the same thing tonight.

MRS. LUPE MARTINEZ had died of a massive heart attack brought on by shock. Gadgets Schwarz might not have M.D. on his list of academic accomplishments, but his hypothesis about the old widow's cause of death was right on target. She had been frightened into cardiac arrest—scared to death.

Death had been instantaneous, according to one of the paramedics who zipped her up in the body bag. "Oh, yeah," he said, nodding as if bored. "The Widow Martinez. She's gone Core on us a couple of times. Three strikes and I guess you're out."

"Doesn't make it any fairer," Gadgets noted somberly.

"Fair?" the ambulance attendant snorted, chuckling. "You want fair? Go to a circus, pal. This is the big city. This is El Paso. You won't find any compassion here."

Turning his back on the self-styled expert, Gadgets exchanged a pained look with Lyons.

"Forget it," he muttered under his breath.

"Already have," Lyons said, brushing his knuckles together as if wiping his hands of the entire unsavory matter. "The paramedic dude's past history, old business."

"Good answer." Gadgets felt relieved. They were good for one another—the three of them. They kept each other healthy—mentally. And that was what it took in this line of work. Combating the world's evils could leave even the toughest crime fighter with more than mere physical wounds.

The Able Team commandos felt obliged to inspect the entire premises before wrapping up their operation, of course, despite the protests of Father Franco and the other elderly priest. Father Felipe just stood in the shadows, arms folded across his chest, watching the cleanup maneuvering.

Uniformed officers checked beneath each pew for abandoned weapons, or any other physical evidence that might assist in the prosecution of the two coyotes-turned-killers from Ciudad Juárez. Plainclothes detectives soon arrived and began taking statements from the officers involved in the pursuit as well as the priests. Six counts of vehicular manslaughter were also laid.

Lyons was the one who tumbled to the secret first. Something seemed to beckon to him, and he found himself drawn to a closed door next to one of the confessionals. He just couldn't help it. The urge was uncontrollable. Motioning Blancanales and Schwarz over to his side, he forced the flimsy deadbolt lock, opening a metal door that creaked appropriately.

"What's that sound?" Blancanales asked, his voice lowered.

Lyons cupped an ear. "What sound?"

"Sounds like a dragon slumbering down there or something," Pol quipped without the routine smirk. "A breathing sound. A *big* breathing sound."

"Cut the crap, will you?" Lyons said, readying his CAR-15 nonetheless.

"Sounds to me like Apples," Schwarz suggested.

"Apples?" Ironman asked, cocking an eyebrow skeptically.

"You're talking Apples of the computer strain," Blancanales guessed, a sparkle in his eyes.

"Maybe IBM," Schwarz said, changing his mind.

"We'll soon find out," Lyons vowed as he crept down the dimly lit stairwell into the underground chamber two full floors beneath the rectory of Saint Michael's.

Once at the bottom, he held his metal flashlight away from his body and pushed the pulse button several times, directing the bursts of light in different directions. There was no sign that anyone was present in the chamber, and he waved his two partners down the stairs one at a time.

If he was expecting a medieval dungeon or torture chamber filled with cobwebs and old skeletons, Lyons was disappointed. Saint Michael's was old—nearly two hundred years—but not *that* old.

Instead, what Able Team found was a long, narrow room barren of any furniture except automated phone banks attached to each wall. A flick of a nearby switch further revealed that the room could be brightly illuminated. The phone banks had been partitioned into individual cubicles. Some were equipped with computer terminals—a few were on even now, their consoles glowing green, blue or yellow. The constant hum of their disk drive fans was the sound Blancanales had heard at the top of the stairwell.

One of the phones began ringing, breaking the tense silence with an old-fashioned dual-bell clang.

"Are we home?" Blancanales quipped.

His old LAPD habits kicking in, Lyons grinned and said, "Why not?" He was thinking about an old narcotics bust in the Wilshire district of Los Angeles. They had raided a known drug kingpin's den, only to have the phone start ringing off the hook while they were still logging evidence and preparing to cart the hooligan from Bogotá off to the station. Instead of allowing it to ring, the detectives had answered it, posing as the dope pusher's gang, Spanish accents and all. The users bought it, hook, line and sinker, and before Lyons's decoy squad wrapped up their operation that evening, they'd lured nearly two dozen potential arrestees to the cocaine distributor's mansion. Since then the scam had been duplicated a thousand times by a hundred different cops working the seamier side of Los Angeles.

Before Lyons could cross the room to pick up the phone, however, a second receiver began ringing. This one had a modern soft-toned buzz to it, and Lyons—still moving toward a distant cubicle—motioned Schwarz to pick it up.

But the rings stopped and answering machines kicked in before either commando could reach a receiver. Blancanales glanced into the nearest cubicle, then another. "Every *one* of these suckers has got an answering machine in it," he said, sounding amazed.

Schwarz glanced at Lyons. "A numbers outfit?"

"Our friends in the clergy?" Lyons gestured toward the stairwell that led back to the three priests still being questioned topside. "I kind of doubt it, Hermann."

He examined one of the answering machines, then gently pressed a button so that they could monitor the message being left. It was in rapid-fire Spanish, lasting less than twenty seconds. "Either of you catch any of that?" Lyons asked, staring at Blancanales.

"I missed some of it," Pol replied.

Schwarz pressed up the monitoring switch on the other answering machine, but the caller had already hung up.

"Play it back," Lyons directed as he walked across the room toward a small black ashtray.

"You got it," Gadgets complied.

"Father Franco," a woman's hushed voice whispered across the phone line, "This is Theresa. Hector is bringing in a vanload from Guatemala at six tomorrow morning."

"Guns maybe?" Schwarz said, glancing back at Lyons, who placed a rigid forefinger against his lips, requesting silence.

"Call me back if you cannot accommodate them. Thank you, and God bless." The woman left her phone number—Lyons recognized it as being a local El Paso exchange—then hung up.

The former L.A. policeman stared down at the black ashtray. A barely noticeable curl of smoke was still rising from a squashed cigarette butt. "This place is a safehouse," he told them. Using only the edges of his fingernails, he picked up the cigarette butt as if it were contaminated.

"A safehouse?" Schwarz questioned, glancing around.

"For illegal aliens," Blancanales said, nodding.

"Right," Lyons agreed as he poked the other cigarette butts lying in the ashtray. "Part of the underground Sanctuary Movement, I'd wager."

"We've got no quarrel with them," Blancanales said. "Though I think they've got their priorities screwed up."

Lyons knew it was Pol's way of saying, "Let's get out of here. We don't need the extra hassle." The Able Team leader grinned. "I'd further wager that one or all of our three priests were down here personally manning the phone banks, then were drawn topside by all the commotion out in the street, or by the sound of the two coyotes' footfalls across the floorboards overhead."

"We're too far down for that," Schwarz disagreed, glancing at the reinforced concrete ceiling above. "Two levels, remember?"

"Whatever," Lyons said, moving toward the stairwell. "Find out which one of those cowboy priests smokes Marlboros," he called up to one of the young uniformed officers crouching beside the door two flights up.

"You guys Code-Four down there?" the rookie yelled back.

"Yeah, sorry," Lyons added. "Everything's secure. Did you hear what I asked you?"

"Roger!" the policeman responded, as if talking on a radio.

Able Team listened to a muffled exchange of words up on ground level then, less than a minute later, the rookie said, "None of them smoke."

"Pat 'em down," Lyons directed, his voice now raised and laced with irritation.

"Do what?" the rookie called down, somewhat incredulously.

"You heard me. Search the good fathers, kid!"

"Uh, right!"

A couple of minutes later an El Paso police sergeant escorted Father Felipe down into the underground chamber. The police sergeant was silent as he held on to the younger priest's right bicep. His gun hand clutched a crumpled pack of Marlboros. The sparkle in the sergeant's eyes spoke volumes—it always pleased him immensely to catch a liar red-handed, especially one wearing the uniform of the Roman Catholic Church, even if he wasn't sure what such a simple deception was leading to.

"Quite an operation you've got here, *Father*," Lyons said, locking eyes with the stone-faced clergyman.

"Any comment to be made about this...this invasion of privacy will come from our attorney." Dwarfed by the big sergeant, Felipe sneered and jerked his arm free. "I'm still waiting to be granted my *right* to make that call."

"You haven't been officially arrested yet," the sergeant said. "But you're coming awful damn close, Father."

"Maintaining a clandestine phone bank doesn't appear to be in violation of any laws that I know of," Lyons said, baiting the priest.

"Then release me and—" Felipe began.

"Unless, of course, you're plotting to overthrow the government or something."

"Nonsense!"

"That's what I thought." Lyons stepped over to one of the answering machines and played back its latest message. A man spoke in slow Spanish for fifteen or twenty seconds, then hung up. Something about Honduras. Lyons maintained eye-to-eye contact with Felipe during the entire playback. "Then again," he said, "harboring illegal aliens *is* a violation of some sort of law *somewhere*, of that I'm sure. Especially if you're giving them menial jobs of any sort, or spending money."

Felipe's face softened somewhat. "The church has always welcomed with open arms those less fortunate than—"

"I'm not here for a sermon, Father," Lyons said, tilting his head slightly to the side, waiting for the admission he wanted to hear.

"That you're here at all, a citizen of the United States—the most prosperous, advanced civilization on the face of the Lord's Earth—is nothing more than an accident of birth, my friend."

Gadgets Schwarz sensed a sudden deterioration in the interrogation. "I'm sure the Immigration and Naturalization Service would be interested in volunteering to 'work' your phone banks for a couple of shifts, pal. On the house, of course."

"Consider it a contribution," Blancanales added, his eyes narrowing as he surveyed the priest's face.

A look of horror had come across the man's features. "You can't be serious!"

"Watch me." Lyons stepped closer to the stairwell and called up to ground level. "Patterson! We've got something hopping down here I think your boys would get off on!"

"Please!" Father Felipe moved closer to Lyons, but the El Paso police sergeant grabbed his arm again. "You're here," he motioned toward Lyons's rifle, and his two shabbily dressed partners, "*whoever* you are." The priest turned to face the sergeant holding his upper arm. "A representative of the El Paso police force is here. There's no need to bring the INS into this. They don't have much of a... sense of humor when it comes to this sort of..." But his voice trailed off.

Lyons scratched at the stubble on his chin. He was always in the mood to negotiate, to barter, swap information or strike a deal. Maybe there was some connection between this Sanctuary Movement operation and the claim that terrorists were moving up through Mexico for an attempted strike at the heart of America. Maybe they were hoping to sneak across the border, posing as illegal *pollos*. Maybe...

A different sort of scratching reached Ironman's sensitive ears. "What was *that*?" he added, whirling to face Blancanales.

"Wasn't me!" Politician said, raising his hands defensively.

Schwarz had heard the sound, too, and was racing over toward one of the computers.

"We've got mice," Father Felipe volunteered, feigning slight embarrassment. "They like to nest in the computer consoles sometimes, for the warmth."

"Mice, my ass," Gadgets said, examining one of the partitions separating a cubicle now. "No offense, Father," he quickly added.

"None taken."

That the priest even bothered to acknowledge Schwarz's comment struck Lyons as suspicious, a bit too condescending. He stared at the man, noticing a nervous tic in one eye.

"Bingo!" Schwarz pulled a false panel back and then immediately shoved at one of the partitions, using the full weight of his body.

An entire cubicle slid aside on well-oiled wheels, and Father Felipe responded with an audible groan. Behind the false wall was another chamber, almost equal in size to the one they now occupied. But the hidden room was crowded with illegal aliens, sitting shoulder to shoulder on rugs or blankets of various colors. The room had likely been darkened the instant Felipe and his fellow priests had left the underground boiler room to investigate the disturbance upstairs.

The *pollos* now squinted against the bright light bathing their faces. Lyons scanned the group: more than thirty males, and a third as many women. There were a few children clustered near a corner in the back, playing with cockroaches tied to long strings. Three or four mothers kept their infants quiet by stuffing the babies' mouths with cold nipples.

A set of handcuffs out, the sergeant from the El Paso PD was already guiding Father Felipe's wrists behind his back.

Lyons listened to the rattle of handcuffs clicking into place. "Take him away," he told the big sergeant. "And the two clergymen upstairs, as well."

Wordlessly the police sergeant nodded, then guided a silent Felipe toward the stairwell.

Patterson rushed down the steps past them as they started up. "What do you have?" he asked.

"When's your birthday?" Lyons countered.

"Not for another seven months," Patterson said, his curious grin warped into a suspicious frown. "Why?"

"Consider this an early present, dude."

5

"Quite a network," Lyons said, flipping through a box stuffed with files.

"I'm impressed," Blancanales agreed.

The men of Able Team, assisted by Patterson and his border patrolmen, quickly discovered that Fathers Franco and Felipe were running more than a sophisticated "underground railroad," designed to ferry illegal aliens to points farther inland, such as Texas, Arizona and New Mexico. From the basement of Saint Michael's they were also supporting a network of Communist sympathizers operating out of the Central American countries of El Salvador, Honduras and Guatemala.

The priests used their bank of phones and computers to coordinate the channeling of funds and supplies to the antigovernment rebels, as well as to smuggle Communist agents north, once their usefulness south of the border began to wane or the scene in El Salvador became too hot.

"Do you think these clowns are connected with the terrorist network Pol's team was on the lookout for back down in Canine Canyon?" Schwarz asked his two partners.

"That would be just a little too easy, don't you think?" Lyons said, cracking a smile as he started in on another box of computer hard copy.

"Yeah, I suppose," Schwarz said, still uncertain.

"Maybe not," Blancanales said, holding a sheaf of printout paper over his head for the other to see. "Check *this* crap out!"

"That's the logo of Red Lance," Lyons informed the group after he'd joined Politician.

"The dudes we were hoping to catch crossing the border at Juárez," Gadgets added. He suddenly looked worried as he, too, examined the crimson stamp of a longhorn bull upright on its hind legs, brandishing a long, oversize lance.

Blancanales frowned. "I'd say they're already in the country."

"Or at least their support base is," Lyons interjected.

"Support base?" Blancanales asked, although he already knew what Lyons would say.

"Sympathetic locals," Ironman said, gritting his teeth. "They could be anybody. Guilt-ridden liberals with a printing press, ex-*pollos* with some extra cocaine money in their pocket to contribute...maybe even hard core elements of KGB-backed—"

"*Most probably* hard-core elements of KGB-backed troublemakers," Blancanales said, finishing the sentence for him.

Gadgets was examining the documents. "No addresses," he said finally. "Not even a phone number."

"It's just propaganda leaflets," Blancanales added as he set the handful of unprofessional brochures down.

"But maybe we *can* find something of use in one of these other file boxes," Lyons said, starting toward the nearest one.

Schwarz gestured at the far wall of the chamber, which had been used to hide the illegal aliens. "There must be a ton of crap in them," he complained. "It'll take weeks."

As he spoke, some of Patterson's men were escorting the last of the handcuffed illegals toward the stairwell. "We could use some of *them*" the senior border patrolman said, gesturing toward a young, attractive *señorita*.

"Get real," Lyons returned.

"I'm serious," Patterson maintained. "They speak Spanish. And they work dirt-cheap."

Lyons forced a laugh. "Shit, how about if we just borrow some of your rookie agents, okay?"

"No problem," Patterson agreed, turning to follow the prisoners upstairs. "Be right back with some recruits," he said.

"*I* thought we'd be kickin' ass and takin' names when Hal sent us to Texas," Blancanales complained when Patterson was gone, "not comparing them with a master manifest from Havana Central."

"You can't always have an eight-and-skate schedule, okay, Pol?" Lyons said, not looking up from his box of alphabetized files. "Sometimes you just gotta *work* for a living."

"Well, there must be a million Martinezes in this file box alone, for Christ's sake."

"Christ ain't interested, and neither am I. Speak to me when you discover something that'll help us crack this case."

"Crack *what* case?" Gadgets asked. "Last I heard, we were mounting a dual operation back at the border—roust some gutless bandits who were preying on the *pollos*, and attempt to intercept a couple of ragtag terrorists wearing ayatollah turbans."

"Nobody said they were Arabs," Lyons said, running the back of his hand across his forehead to wipe small beads of perspiration away. "I mean, Iranians." His slip elicited a chuckle from both Blancanales and Schwarz. Finally Ironman's mental defenses broke down, and he laughed along. "Shit, you guys!"

Schwarz persisted. "It wasn't a *case*. It was busywork, and you know it."

"I doubt Brognola just wanted to get us out of his hair or—" Lyons began.

"They always send the hopeless cases down to the Mexican border," Blancanales said, winking. "Don't you two watch television?"

"Not if I can avoid it," Lyons snorted.

All eyes rose as a collection of footfalls started down the stairwell, bringing an unceremonious halt to the verbal jousting.

"Here," Patterson said, presenting Lyons with two young Hispanic officers. "They're all yours for the rest of the shift, until end of watch."

"Do they speak Spanish?" Lyons asked. "I mean, *fluent* Spanish? Like a *pollo*?"

"Is the Pope Polish?" Patterson countered.

Lyons turned to face Blancanales. "I don't know—is he?"

"Search me," Pol answered, extending a handshake to the nearest border patrolman, noting that his name tag read Lanno. He waved a hand at the long line of computerized phone banks. "Welcome to the hell-hole, kid." The other agent's name was Zamora. "Now, I'll show you what we want you to—"

No sooner had Politician started over toward the nearest Magnavox console than two phones began ringing. "Go to it," Schwarz told the nervous-looking rookies.

"What do we say?"

"Just fake it," Blancanales answered, although he wasn't looking very confident himself. "Pretend you're selling subscriptions to some magazine or something, then see where the conversations lead."

"I didn't join the Border Patrol to get into phone sales," one of the rookies complained as he took a seat before a ringing phone.

Blancanales folded his arms across his chest and took a deep breath as if to psyche himself up. "The constant battle to thwart America's ever-present enemies often take strange twists, my man,'' he said, releasing the air from his lungs in a long, drawn-out sigh.

The five of them worked through the ensuing daylight hours, taking three- or four-hour sleep breaks on an alternating basis until the sun went down again. When Patterson returned at 2200 hours in a fresh uniform to check on their progress, Able Team and the two Border Patrol rookies had logged nearly a hundred incoming phone calls. Almost a third of the callers had hung up at the sound of unfamiliar voices. Another third stated that they believed they'd reached wrong numbers. The remainder called to confirm that carloads of illegal aliens from the Juárez line were inbound.

The INS kept a fleet of cage buses parked in the back to ferry the startled arrivals back to a customs checkpoint for free mug shots and random fingerprinting, depending on the need for routine attitude adjustments.

The woman identifying herself as Theresa called back again, wondering what had happened to Hector. Hector had, of course, been promptly arrested for transporting illegal aliens upon his arrival at Saint Michael's, but Lyons didn't tell her this. Instead, he claimed that Hector had never arrived. Her tone remaining carefree, Theresa thanked Lyons cordially and, again, ended the conversation with, "*Gracias . . .* and God bless."

There were no phone calls from terrorists, junior apprentice zealots or even armchair fellow travelers. No secret agents. Not even a single clown in a Zapata mustache claiming to be with Castro or the KGB. For the most part, Blancanales and Schwarz logged the whole fiasco down as a total loss. "Chalk it up to experience," Gadgets muttered. "I guess."

Lyons wasn't as pessimistic. "Give it time," he said.

Meanwhile, a couple of old friends of Hal Brognola, who held revered positions in the hierarchy of the El Paso PD, managed to temporarily close Saint Michael's on the basis that it was a public nuisance. It was the first time in the state's history that a house of worship had been so labeled.

There was a short write-up and a grainy black-and-white photo in the Metro section of the city's daily newspaper. The article reported that several suspected illegal aliens had lost their lives in a bizarre traffic accident in front of Saint Michael's Church, but nothing was said about the church's clergymen, or the fact that all subsequent masses at the parish had been temporarily canceled.

Lyons was grateful that it was now Monday. The only traditional churchgoers his people had had to deal with were the daily diehards who attended the 6:00 a.m. mass— barely more than a dozen elderly women. They didn't argue when plainclothes agents from the INS turned them away, but merely returned home to light candles for the priests who they'd been told had come down with Taiwan flu.

As midnight approached, Able Team opened their last file box in the basement of the church.

"I'm tellin' you," Schwarz muttered. "This is going to be a bust. Why don't we just chuck this sucker and—"

"I've always had good luck toward the *end* of my investigations," Lyons insisted. "Hang in there. Remember— we're looking for anything that can officially tie those priests into Red Lance. Or anything identifying the members of Red Lance. Or anything involving the group itself."

"Or anything juicy on people whose name I'd recognize," Gadgets reminded Pol. "I still can't believe we found Kathy-Joe Travis's name in those files."

"And *I* can't believe you listen to *that* brand of folk music," Lyons said, taunting him about the little-known singer.

"Once in a while," Schwarz admitted sheepishly.

"It's country and western devil worship, dude," Blancanales said, laughing. "Pure and simple. Steer away from the chick, man, I'm telling you."

"Bull, too," Schwarz snapped.

"Just about," Pol agreed, smirking.

"I just can't believe she's a member of Red Lance," Schwarz said, shaking his head.

"The file just said she made a contribution to the cause," Lyons reminded him. "Nothing about her being a card-carrying member. Let's keep a grip on reality here."

The sound of a horn honking beyond the walls upstairs brought instant silence to the room. Although there were two border patrolmen and a token El Paso police officer maintaining a security "static post" just inside the church's main entrance, all eyes glanced up the open stairwell in anticipation.

The horn sounded again, this time with a long, drawn-out racket that could easily be heard two floors down. "I'll check it out," Lyons said, grabbing one of the CAR-15s leaning against the nearest wall.

"I'll back your sorry ass," Blancanales said automatically.

"We'll keep the bench warm," Schwarz cracked, concentrating on a file.

Outside, Patterson was climbing into a Border Patrol Jeep that had come to pick him up. Lyons had assumed he'd gone long ago, but it turned out the senior patrolman had actually spent the past hour or so exchanging the latest rumors and agency lowdown with the three men posted at the entrance.

"What's up?" Ironman asked, his eyes focused on the black strip of neatly trimmed tape across Patterson's badge—the universal sign of mourning among cops for a fallen brother.

There had been an officer-involved shooting south of the Juárez checkpoint. Another decoy team, dispatched by the

El Paso office, had confronted more bandits preying on *pollos* a hundred yards or so *north* of the border, *inside* U.S. territory.

Three coyotes were reported dead.

"Got to get down there and show 'em how to do the paperwork," Patterson said, winking at Lyons as he climbed into the passenger side of the Border Patrol unit.

"That's *one* thing I don't miss about law enforcement," Ironman said, nodding, his mind flashing back to his days with the LAPD as he watched the Jeep's shock absorbers sink under the big agent's weight. He'd always been three or four days late turning in his reports—even on some felony arrests. The bad habit hadn't endeared him to many patrol sergeants, but they had tended to overlook the practice in light of Lyons's reputation as a man who could be more than counted on when outnumbered street cops in some back alley or dark building called for help. Carl was usually the first backup unit on-scene, even when he had to race across town, Code-Three.

"Catch you clowns later," Patterson said, treating them to a casual half salute as the Renegade Jeep pulled away.

"That piece of shit needs a tune-up!" Lyons called after the Jeep, which was being driven by Cooper.

"It didn't need one until after *you* got done running it into the ground," the border patrolman yelled back at Ironman.

"Think he was upset about those two rods I threw last night?" Lyons asked Blancanales as the Jeep's red taillights faded in the mist.

"Forget him if he can't take a joke," Politician answered, slapping his partner on the back as they headed back down into the concrete bowels of the dark church.

Curiously the phone calls coming into the Sanctuary Movement headquarters dropped to a trickle soon after Lyons and Blancanales returned to the underground phone bank below Saint Michael's. At 3:00 a.m. the men from

Able Team challenged their two border patrolmen to a game of cards, but the rookies weren't as green as they looked. Spotting conspiracy in the eyes of Gadgets and Politician, they bowed out gracefully, claiming that Patterson insisted they compile copious notes regarding the priests' files and write up an after-action synopsis before the supervisor returned again at dawn.

"What action?" Blancanales snorted, frowning with contempt as he flipped the edge of his thumb over a pack of "Death from Above" playing cards.

The other two commandos from Stony Man Farm eyed Pol suspiciously, glancing down at his legendary ace of spades with its Vietnamese inscription, "Kill Communists" in English and shook their heads in resignation. Shrugging, all three returned to the stacks of files. There was no further talk of a card game that night, although Politician threatened to teach Gadgets how to play Fifty-two Pickup more than a couple of times.

As 4:30 a.m. approached, Schwarz glanced over the shoulders of Patterson's two rookies. They had separated the files into three stacks: financial contributors, possible Red Lance suspects and miscellaneous names that weren't immediately identifiable or easily categorized.

Zamora and Lanno were attacking their tasks diligently, and the sight of them going through file after file without pause reminded Pol of his own youth and the first assignments the government had given him—make-work jobs that he had, nonetheless, poured his heart and soul into. As the years became decades and time in the field quickly passed, he found one thing amusing: there were many things Able Team no longer took seriously. Life and death matters were shrugged off on a routine basis. If their time came, then it came. There was little one could do about it beyond the routine precautions every cop and soldier took to ensure survival in the wild—be it rain forest or urban jungle.

In contrast to the enthusiasm of Zamora and Lanno, Blancanales and Lyons were catching up on their beauty sleep. Both reclined in hard-backed chairs propped against a nearby wall, their boots balanced precariously on top of glowing computer consoles. Meanwhile, Schwarz was attempting to crack password codes that protected certain files on the computer software. His ultimate goal was to introduce a destructive electronic "virus" that would destroy critical components of the software, yet leave other elements of the data bank intact.

A crash of wooden splinters somewhere beyond the top of the stairwell on the ground floor level made Gadgets and his two official assistants freeze.

Shoulders tensing, Schwarz's ears perked up as he listened to a clamor of footfalls overhead. "Sounds like one of the side doors," he growled, lifting the CAR-15 balanced across his thighs. With his other hand he tossed a wadded-up piece of paper at Lyons.

It bounced off Ironman's forehead and came to rest in the crook of Blancanales's neck, effectively waking both men, who had only been dozing on the edge of sleep anyway.

"Upstairs," Schwarz told them, motioning in that direction. "I'd wager an intruder or two has—"

"No such thing as intruders in a church," Lyons said sarcastically, but he, too, moved toward the other assault rifles.

Voices carried down the stairwell. "*Hey!* You guys can't come in here without—"

Gadgets recognized one of the border patrolmen's voices topside. But the challenge was met with a burst of automatic weapons fire.

"Uzi," Lyons yelled, dropping to one knee behind a humming IBM laptop computer that sat on a counter.

6

"Yep, definitely an Uzi!" Gadgets Schwarz agreed, scanning the equipment-filled basement, wondering if it would become their tomb. "An Uzi or a MAC-10 on rock and roll."

Blancanales nodded. "Four sets of footsteps up there," he added.

"No return fire from the good guys," Schwarz commented, as he took cover behind a printer table and motioned the two border patrolmen to do likewise. He glanced at Politician as both men drew back the charging handles on their weapons. The bolts slammed forward with a satisfying clang, and Blancanales grinned, but Gadgets remained grim-faced, wondering how many additional casualties they'd taken topside. "An engine block, it *ain't*!" he said, thrusting his chin at Pol's choice for cover—a bulky fixed-disk computer.

Blancanales's smile faded as he turned a dial on the wall above his head that brought the lights down low. "It'll have to do."

No additional gunshots followed the initial burst from upstairs, but the border patrolmen's authoritative commands for the intruders to drop their weapons were being drowned out by frantic shouts from four people stumbling in a frantic, unorganized rush down the stairwell.

"This is it," Lyons said, bringing his rifle's front sight up. "Get that pistol out of its holster, Lanno," he whispered harshly at the young INS agent. Zamora already had his gun arm extended and braced across a desktop, bone-white knuckles wrapped around a blue-steel revolver.

The first person to reach the basement was a grubby white male in his late thirties, brown hair and beard both falling halfway to his waist. Round wire-rim glasses seemed to keep his bulging eyes inside their sockets. He wore a red-and-black plaid shirt, and his blue jeans were tucked into the tops of recently purchased hiking boots. Though quite slender, he was tall and sported big fists, one of which cradled the Uzi submachine gun they'd heard being fired upstairs. Smoke still curled from its powder-blackened, stubby barrel.

"I told you not to bring that damn thing!" the woman racing down the stairs behind the gunman yelled in a reprimanding tone. "You're going to get us all *killed*, Francis!"

Remaining silent and frozen, Lyons stared at the woman's features. She was probably around the same age as the gunman. Her hair was long and streaked with gray, however, and her spectacles were obviously prescription sunglasses. She wore a long blue calico skirt and a bleached psychedelic T-shirt—the type Carl hadn't seen since he'd stumbled into a coffee shop in Berkeley back in the sixties.

Behind the woman were two more men: one probably American, the other Hispanic. Both had medium-length dark hair and were clean shaven. They wore jeans and bright T-shirts, proclaiming Freedom for Garza across the front in neon pink.

Lyons instantly recognized the name. John Mauricio Garza had been arrested in downtown El Paso a few weeks earlier for killing a local policeman during a foot chase after a convenience store robbery. Radical "brown power" factions in the local Hispanic community had rallied to Garza's defense despite eyewitness accounts claiming the holdup man had circled back on his white pursuer and shot

the twenty-year veteran of the El Paso PD in the back. The
vicious murder left a police widow to raise the dead officer's four sons on her own. It didn't seem to matter to the
press, or Garza's followers, that the patrolman's wife was
of Mexican ancestry herself. She was now a naturalized
American citizen but was originally from Tijuana.

"You should have left that damn thing back at the safehouse!" the woman insisted again, thrusting her chin back
at the others, as well. "*All* of you should have!"

"The world has changed, Cecilia!" the gunman began,
rambling incoherently. "It's no longer the Age of Aquar-
ius. No longer the 'time of the seasons,' baby! We can't
place sunflowers in The Man's rifle barrels anymore. We've
got to carry the cold metal ourselves...make the point! *Get
them to listen to us!* Can you *dig it*, girl?"

Blancanales glanced over at Lyons. Both men rolled their
eyeballs toward the ceiling: this was going to be as easy as
rousting a gang of dopeheads at a toke party.

"You certainly got their attention this time, Francis!" the
woman said, throwing a clenched fist at the gunman,
striking him between the shoulder blades as they both finally reached the bottom of the stairwell and moved into
the empty space in the middle of the room.

"I don't think you hit any of them!" the Hispanic
shouted. "You just really pissed them off, man!"

"Of course I wasn't trying to *shoot* anybody!" the man
called Francis argued, throwing up his hands. "I was just
trying to make...a...*point*!"

He aimed the Uzi at a dimly glowing light fixture and
pulled the trigger, but there was no discharge.

"Swift, Sherlock!" The woman sighed as she dropped
into a nearby chair. "Now what? You make us follow you
into Saint Mike's, then you shoot up some stained glass
windows and—"

"Then he leads us like trapped rats down into the belly
of a sinking ship," the American wearing the Freedom

T-shirt said, speaking up for the first time as his eyes scanned the top of the stairwell and he reached for something tucked inside his waistband. "After shooting up the town! And for what?"

"To make a point, fool!" Francis answered, glaring at the younger man.

Cecilia was nodding, as if remembering the party line for the first time. "I guess he's right, damn it!" she told the others, though her own tone sounded less than convinced. "We have to stand up for Father Felipe and the others! If *we* don't, who will? They've got the goddamn INS up there. This is a church! This is *sanctuary*! And they've got border cops and El Paso pigs trampling about up there, leaving their filth on . . . on holy ground!"

From the top of the stairwell voices called down, "Lyons! Schwarz! You guys okay down there? We've got reinforcements on the way! We'll have this place sealed up tighter than a—"

"What's he talking about?" Francis demanded as he rushed toward one of the light switches. His eyes scanned the dimly lit room as he moved, free hand struggling to remove the Uzi's empty magazine.

"Jump his ass!" Lyons called to Blancanales, who was closer.

The directive was unnecessary. Pol, a former black beret in Southeast Asia, was already flying through the air, pantherlike.

He smashed against the intruder's midsection with a powerful body block. The Uzi clattered to the floor and slid across the concrete like fingernails down a chalkboard.

The man with long hair grunted, slammed backward into the nearest wall and collapsed, the wind knocked from his lungs. His wire-rim glasses slid down to the tip of his nose, and a startled look glazed his eyes as they locked onto Blancanales's.

"On your belly, buddy!" Pol yelled, although his actions didn't match the mock courtesy as he latched on to the man's hair and twirled him over, facedown, against the cold floor.

Schwarz tackled the woman in record time, separating her from the others, grabbing her wrist and jerking her out of the line of fire and into the shadows as Lyons rushed toward the two men sliding down the stairwell railing behind her. But Ironman wasn't fast enough.

The closest opponent's left hand was up now, and a short-barreled revolver pointed directly at the stone-faced commando's chest. Lyons pivoted, dropped and swung around, all in the same blink of an eye. His right foot came up, missed the Colt .38, but connected with a shin. His heel ricocheted up into the man's groin as the Able Team warrior dropped onto his side, absorbing the fall's impact with a slapping motion of elbow and wrist, martial-arts style, against the unyielding concrete.

The Colt .38 discharged, sending a soft-nosed slug into the concrete ceiling. The bullet bounced back down with an earsplitting crack, flattening out between them like a squashed, misshapen beetle stopped by a windshield.

Having cheated death or serious injury by a whisper of time, Lyons didn't pause to ponder his luck or count his blessings. He twisted again, his opposite foot flying out and seeking the second man, trying to connect. But the last target was too far away.

And he was armed, as well.

Halfway off the stairwell's bottom step, the man leaned back as if trying to avoid all contact with strangers who had infiltrated the Sanctuary Movement's headquarters.

Behind Lyons, Schwarz had his hands full. The woman had erupted into a wildcat, striking out at him with all four limbs. Though she inflicted little damage, she succeeded in creating considerable interference, forcing Gadgets to both fend off blows to the face and protect his private parts from knee jabs and vicious kicks. Finally he simply ended her show of bravado with a swift punch to the chin. Thankfully the woman had a glass jaw, and she went down like a rifle-shot deer as the last man on the stairwell produced—and aimed—a compact .380 automatic of his own.

Unleashing a 10-round burst from the hip, Gadgets held the CAR-15 ready until several seconds after the gunman collapsed at the foot of the stairs. The man's chest cavity was properly ventilated, his eyes lifeless as they stared through the electronics wizard from Stony Man Farm.

Rolling smoke rings rising from his rifle barrel, Schwarz finally lowered the weapon and started over toward the nearest pistol—a revolver Lyons's tackle had dropped on the way down. He kicked it to the far side of the room, then retrieved the .380 auto from the subject whose ticket he'd just canceled. Glancing over in Ironman's direction, he saw that Lyons had confiscated the empty Uzi, while Blancanales had handcuffed one intruder and was rolling the semiconscious woman onto her stomach so that he could pin her wrists behind her back with flexi-cuffs.

"Hey! What's the score down there?" a border patrolman called down the smoke-laced stairwell.

"We're okay!" his fellow INS agent advised, voice cracking slightly. "Four in custody—one posthumously."

"Acknowledged!" There was no hiding the excitement in the other officer's voice. This had been his first shootout, albeit a somewhat one-sided affair. Oh, he had been in other confrontations before—especially down on the border, where rock-throwing contests between *pollos* and checkpoint agents were an almost weekly occurrence. But a genuine, bona fide stint of gunplay! And *indoors* no less! Now *that* was something to phone home about.

Able Team spent the next couple of minutes dragging their prisoners over to the wall against the stairwell, where they were lined up, backs against the beige stucco. The man named Francis stared up at Lyons, an uncomprehending glaze still clouding his eyes. Cecilia groaned now and then as she leaned over slightly to one side, trying to rub her bruised chin. Her eyes remained tightly closed. The third survivor stared straight ahead, avoiding eye contact with the commandos who had invaded Saint Michael's Church without invitation.

"So what do we do with these scum bags?" the INS agent crouching over Schwarz's victim asked as he glanced back over one shoulder.

"Stuff him," Lyons said coldly. "Then mount him and hang him on the wall, bud."

"Huh?" A bit of a youthful innocence left the young border patrolman's wide eyes.

"'There is no hunting like the hunting of man,'" Schwarz said, quoting Ernest Hemingway without premeditation. "'And those who have hunted armed men long enough, and enjoyed it, never care for anything else thereafter....'"

"Say what?" the INS agent asked, cocking an eyebrow.

"Aw, nothing," Gadgets said, blinking, as if to break the spell.

"'You have never lived until you have almost died,'" Blancanales added before flashing a death's-head grin at the bewildered patrolman as he recited an old foxhole phrase popular back in Nam. "'For those who fight for it, life has a flavor the protected will never know.' Welcome to the club, brother."

Starting to comprehend, the young agent finally reholstered his pistol. "But I didn't drop the hammer on this asshole," he argued, as if to protest the soldier's label. "*You* did." He locked eyes with Schwarz as his expression shifted from one of mild awe to serious concern about his own mental faculties.

"Forget it, kid," Blancanales said, dismissing the brief session with a shrug. "Sometimes we just get a little jaded by all the gunsmoke in the air, the cordite lining our lungs. You know?"

"Jaded by choice," Lyons muttered as he began removing ammo magazines from their opponents' weapons.

"Some call it slow poison," Blancanales countered with serious eyes.

"You guys are *too* much," the INS agent said, tilting his head to the other side. "Patterson warned me about you, but I thought he was just kidding. I thought he was full of it. Well, he obviously wasn't."

"What did he say?" Schwarz asked, genuinely curious.

"He said you were bad news." The border patrolman's nervous swallow was loud enough to be heard by everyone in the now quiet-as-a-tomb basement. "That you were some hotshot super commandos from Washington, D.C., and that I'd better cover my ass, because you were nothing but trouble."

"You'll get over it," Schwarz said, smiling for the first time since firing his gun.

"Screw him if he can't take a joke," Lyons said, referring to Patterson.

"Which, I guess, brings me to my original question," the younger patrolman added, shaking his head as the drama deepened and confusion finally set in. "What do we do with these scum bags now?"

"What every good cop worth his weight in Sam Browne leather would do," Lyons answered, motioning toward the portable radio hanging from the border patrolman's belt. "Book 'em, Lanno."

"Uh, right," the agent said, his eyes narrowing.

"Aggravated assault," Ironman said. Then, quickly thinking over what had just transpired, he added, "Make that Attempt 187 on a peace officer."

"Aha!" Zamora's expression brightened. "You guys *are* cops!"

"Nope," Blancanales said, his forehead dipping slightly as he locked eyes with the border patrolman. "But you two rooks are. Remember? You tap-danced on the wrong side of the firing range as well, didn't you?"

"Uh, right twice."

"Dancing with death is sufficient," Blancanales muttered, quoting his favorite dragon lady, Saigon's Madame Nhu, currently living in Parisian exile.

"Now that I think about it," Lyons began, staring at the dead man and the pool of blood on the concrete floor at the foot of the stairs, "I guess the charge would be murder one. Even though the dearly departed was one of their own." Ironman rubbed at the stubble on his pronounced chin. "Yeah, special circumstances, too. Though I'm not quite sure what crime they were planning to commit here, and I haven't come close to deciding what the special circumstances are, except that *we're* here."

"And we're *special*," Schwarz said, expanding his chest importantly despite the manufactured femininity of his tone. Neither of his two cohorts even attempted to match his smile, however.

"Special circumstances would make them eligible for the death penalty," Lanno agreed, nodding.

"Give the man a lollipop for that answer," Gadgets said, staring coldly at the two INS agents. His smile had already faded.

Zamora turned and moved toward the man Cecilia had addressed as Francis. He grabbed hold of the prisoner's upper arms and hoisted him to his feet. "Come on, punk. Off to the monkey house with you."

Smirking, Schwarz said, as he started toward the stairwell, "I'll help with the paperwork."

"That's a big negative," Lyons interjected. "Radio for some uniforms from the El Paso PD to take them off our hands. Later I'll stop by police headquarters personally to see how the truth-or-consequences interrogation session is going. In the meantime we all remain in place, checking these files, monitoring the phones." He turned to face Lanno. "In fact, I could use a few *more* of your people from Immigration and Naturalization," he said. "Something tells me things around here in the wild, wild West are going to start hopping once the sun breaks the eastern horizon."

Zamora sighed loudly. "They haven't already been hopping enough for you three spooky-tunes types?" he challenged, eyes shifting to take in the entire Able Team trio.

"Just think, kid," Lyons said, answering the taunt with a tidbit of insight the rookie would think about on and off for the next couple of weeks. "Only twenty-nine years and some odd months before you're eligible for retirement."

While they waited for the arrival of an El Paso unit for prisoner transport, Blancanales took their Hispanic arrestee aside and, with Lanno's help, convinced the young man to spill the beans. Francis and Cecilia had clammed up the moment their mental faculties returned.

Behind the closed door of the room in which the illegal aliens had hidden, the youth identified himself as Bennie Santana Rodriguez. Because he paused to ponder each individual question asked him and made faces that ran the gamut from extremely comical to severely sad during each mental bout with his conscience, Lyons took to calling him Bennie the Face. He admitted that he was in the country without permission and that Francis and Cecilia were sympathetic to both the Sanctuary Movement and Red Lance. He suspected that the first names they used were as phony as the license plates on their VW van. He also knew little about Red Lance—he'd only been with the group for a week.

Although Bennie didn't have a good grasp of English, when questioned in his native tongue, it became quite apparent that he was both intelligent and articulate. Which, of course, put Blancanales automatically on guard: Pol had been sweet-talked and outmaneuvered by smooth-talking captives in the past, female *and* male. It was a hard way to learn a lesson, and Pol didn't plan on enduring the painfully humiliating experience again.

Francis and Cecilia were, of course, clean—no identification papers whatsoever. Francis had a roll of twenty-dollar bills held together with a rubber band in his front pocket—340 dollars total. Cecilia was carrying two magazines for a .45-caliber pistol taped to the small of her back beneath her blouse. They couldn't locate a Colt automatic to go with them either on her person or in the beat-up Volkswagen van they had used that night for transportation. It was currently parked in a narrow alleyway behind the church, awaiting a police tow and impound.

"From what I've learned," Bennie told Blancanales and Lanno, "Francis and Cecilia are shacking up. They're both anti-U.S. government, anticapitalists—sympathetic to any socialist fad in style. This year it's the Sanctuary Movement. And Red Lance."

"Isn't there *anything* you can tell us about this Red Lance organization?" Blancanales asked.

"I already told you that I'm not really sure just what—"

"You certainly were willing to *die* for Red Lance a few minutes ago," Lanno argued, thrusting his chin in the direction of the blanket-covered body still lying at the foot of the stairs.

"I was earning a paycheck," Bennie argued. "Nothing more. I'm good with guns. I've earned money that way before."

"People don't pack heat unless they're ready and willing to use it," Blancanales said. "Not unless they're incredibly *stupid*. And you don't strike me as being of that species, *amigo*. Now level with us. Maybe we'll talk plea bargain with the local district attorney."

Bennie the Face swallowed hard but refused to break eye contact with Blancanales. "Look, all I know is that they've got this safehouse on the other side of the interstate. A real shitty place. *I* wouldn't even live there, man, and I've dropped my hat just about *anywhere*."

When neither Blancanales nor Lanno made any remarks about that, Bennie continued. "Anyway, they seem to make a lot of phone calls, mail out a lot of propaganda flyers, attend all the rallies, you know.... But mainly they make a lot of phone calls...like they're monitoring the activities of other people in their group, okay?"

"What are you trying to tell us, Bennie, my man?" Pol pressed.

"W-well, I got the impression there was more than one church like this one—more than one place where illegals were being warehoused until they could be ferried north."

"That's common knowledge," Lyons snapped, joining the interrogation. The look on his face told Rodriguez that the commando with ice-blue eyes wasn't impressed.

"Tonight I guess one of your people answered the phone here instead of whoever was *supposed* to answer the phone," Bennie said.

"The priests," Blancanales supplied.

"Yeah, anyway, Francis just about blew a gasket. Ordered us all into the van, and we beat it over here and charged through a side entrance. We got the surprise of our lives when we saw *border* cops sitting inside the church, drinking coffee, let me tell you! And then—"

"Who did you expect to find?" Lyons interrupted.

"Well..." Rodriguez hesitated, his eyes moving from man to man. "I'm not really sure what he—"

"*Tell* us," Lyons ordered, leaning forward. There was no need to flex his impressive biceps, the no-nonsense gleam in his eyes was intimidating enough.

"We sort of expected to find..." It was obvious Bennie was formulating a lie as he spoke. "Well, another faction of Red Lance guys had taken over down here. You know, converted the computers and phone lines to their own purposes—away from that of the Sanctuary Movement.''

Lyons's grin was a tight one. "You're lying to me, Bennie. You're lying through that mile-wide gap in your teeth.''

"I shit you not, man," the young Mexican said, thrusting his chin out at Ironman.

"No, no," Lyons said, getting to his feet and pacing the room. "You're bullshitting ol' Carl to the max. There's something wrong here...something bad going down, and I aim to find out just what—''

His words were interrupted by a ringing from one of the many phones cluttering the basement. "Who in hell would be awake, making phone calls at *this* time of the morning?" Schwarz asked, glancing at the wall clock that read 5:30 a.m.

"Only cops, crooks and other assorted crazies," Lyons informed him, motioning for Blancanales to pick up the receiver.

"Saint Michael's," Politician answered on the third ring. "May we help you with—''

He was cut off by an angry woman with a deep, rasping voice, also speaking in Spanish. Twice as fast, however, and with considerably more vehemence. Even Lyons and Schwarz could hear her shouts from several feet away. The room fell silent in anticipation.

Blank-faced, Blancanales returned the receiver to its cradle after a loud click signaled the end of the one-sided conversation. He turned to face Gadgets and Ironman, a mixed look of intrigue and foreboding lining his dark eyes.

"Well?" Lyons questioned, folding his arms across his chest and shifting into an impress-me stance.

"Some woman..." Blancanales began.

"We heard," Schwarz said, his grin tight and tentative.

"Claims she's with the Salvadoran secret police.''

"What?" Lyons demanded.

"Yeah. Claims they know all about the priests at Saint Michael's and the Sanctuary Movement and all the misguided 'peasants' working here to harbor illegal aliens fleeing Central America. Claims that every volunteer working for Fathers Franco and Felipe is marked for death."

"What was that last part all about?" Lyons asked. "I could hear it clear over here—sounded like a college cheer or something!"

Politician's face grew somber. "Not quite. Roughly translated, she was proclaiming that, 'The death squad has arrived in El Paso!'"

7

"This van reminds me of my high school buddy," Schwarz announced as the Border Patrol unit cruised south on Highway 54 back toward the international checkpoint separating Texas from Mexico. An INS barracks and six hours of sleep awaited them there. Gadget's words broke a tense silence that had filled the vehicle ever since it had pulled away from gloomy Saint Michael's in downtown El Paso.

"I think we've heard this one before," Lyons said, pointing his finger as if preparing to put Schwarz out of his nostalgic misery.

"No, we haven't," Blancanales countered as Ironman drew his pistol and then used his other hand to produce a brown-and-purple jeweler's dust cloth from a back pocket. He began wiping down the pistol's long blue steel barrel.

"Anyway," Schwarz continued, sensing their discontent but pressing on, "my buddy had this really cool van...."

"Really cool?" Lyons parroted, smirking.

"Roger that. Just about as cool as you, Ironman," Gadgets returned, matching his pal's derisive mask.

"I'm sure," Lyons said, glancing forward at Lanno and Zamora, who were riding up front. Agent Lanno sat behind the steering wheel.

"He's too hip for us," Blancanales joked, elbowing Schwarz lightly.

"Anyway," the electronics wizard continued, undaunted, "my buddy had this van, and the chicks loved it, see? So we'd cruise past the school on Fridays after classes and challenge some of the rather ripe and overly endowed cheerleaders to get in and accompany us out to the edge of town into the boonies. We'd usually get three or four girls to go with us and we'd park beside this bend in the river where it was real shallow. And we'd wade across to this small island in the middle of the river...."

"You'd *wade* across?" Lyons challenged. "Couldn't have been a *genuine* river, dude. Couldn't have been an *American* river. Must have been a real *wimpy* river, right, Rosario?"

Schwarz started to argue, but thought better of it at the last moment. When Blancanales remained silent, he continued. "So we'd make our way over to this island, build us a truly righteous campfire, toast marshmallows and bake potatoes wrapped in tinfoil until the sun went down."

"You'd sit out there on that island all afternoon, waiting for the sun to go down?" Lyons asked, finally glancing up. "What for?"

"For the full moon to come out."

"Why?" Lyons questioned, tilting his head to one side and crossing his eyes in mock anticipation.

"Because the broads wouldn't go skinny-dipping in the shallows until it got dark, dumbo."

Both Lyons and Blancanales stared at Schwarz with blank faces. Their eyes requested a moral to the story, but Gadgets couldn't provide one.

Sensing this, Pol said, "Screw it. Don't mean nothing. What the hell's your point?"

"It's just that," Schwarz mumbled. "I mean, well...this old beat-up van just reminded me of back then, that's all. Life didn't seem so...so complicated back then, you know? It was more carefree...more easygoing."

"Yeah," Lyons said, chuckling coldly. "The vulnerable years."

"When papa was paying all the bills," Blancanales reminded Gadgets. "When your old man made sure there was a roof over your head and junk food in the fridge."

"Everything was so much simpler," Schwarz mused. "Back then—"

"Wish you were back there?" Blancanales asked, jabbing Gadgets in the side with a rifle barrel. "Beside the river with the cheerleaders and their pom-poms?"

"Hell, no," Schwarz replied without hesitation. "I *hated* high school, man."

"Shit." Lyons exhaled loudly as he reholstered his side arm. "Sometimes you're so full of hot wind, Gadgets."

"But I thought—" Blancanales began.

"I was just saying how this van brought back some memories, man, that's all," Schwarz added defensively.

Blancanales switched subjects as if changing ammo in a banana clip from tracer to hollowpoint. "You think that caller was pulling a prank?" he asked Ironman. "The one claiming she's with a death squad and that the death squad's done come to town?"

"It's hard to say," Lyons responded dryly. "This case has been unpredictable since it began. Why *not* invite the Salvadoran secret police to join in on the fun? Why *not* welcome the death squad with open arms?"

"I guess *we* don't have anything to worry about," Schwarz said. "After all, the government of El Salvador is an American ally, right? They're on *our* side."

"Last I heard," Lyons said, frowning.

A loud, garbled transmission from the police radio hanging from the dashboard broke the silence after Lyons's ambiguous comments.

"Don't tell me," Ironman said, hanging his head. "Someone clear over on the other side of town is calling for help, and *we* get to respond, right?"

Lanno responded with an easy laugh. "Naw," he said, reaching down to turn up the static-filled transmission. "I've got this sucker on scan. It's picking up one of the El Paso PD's emergency bands. Seems they've got some kind of major-crime activity going on over on the north side of town."

Their eyes equally heavy with fatigue, Blancanales and Lyons exchanged tense glances. "Major crime?" Rosario asked.

Lanno didn't immediately elaborate. He was cruising along at sixty miles an hour down the freeway, head lowered to the edge of the dashboard as he fiddled with the radio's channel scanner. "Sounds like a shooting."

Schwarz's eyes rolled up toward the van's ceiling. "Let it be two drunk cowboys shooting it out on Main Street," he quietly pleaded with whichever deity might be watching over Able Team today.

Lyons stared out at the sizzling orb of a sun as it finally rose above the eastern horizon. As its appearance filled him with warmth, the drained feeling of exhaustion seemed to fade, although Ironman was still left with a gnawing emptiness in his gut.

Dawn.

He'd always hated it. Sunrise signaled the end of the graveyard shift when he'd worked with the LAPD. But once the sun came up, regardless of how sleepy he'd felt since the bars closed and the action died down, his fatigue was always replaced with a hollow restlessness that remained with him even when he'd crawled into bed. Now he stared at the early-morning sun and sensed that their duty shift was far from over.

Lanno had switched the monitor to a car-to-car frequency, and they listened to the first units arriving at the shooting scene.

"Better get paramedics up here ASAP!" one patrolman requested urgently.

"What's your status?" a watch commander asked, his siren filling the background with harsh electronic yelps as he squealed around a corner, engine roaring.

"It's the alley in back of Assumption Church, off McKelligon Canyon Road," the officer answered. "The shooter's GOA, Sarge!" Gone on arrival.

"How many victims?"

"Eight, over."

"Eight?"

"Ten-four. All illegals, it appears. Somebody mowed 'em down with a machine gun."

"Shit," Lyons said, rubbing his throbbing temples.

"Is Assumption Church affiliated in any way with—" Blancanales began to ask the driver, but Lanno had already anticipated the question.

"We've suspected the priests there were part of the Sanctuary Movement for quite some time now," he affirmed.

"You better take us up there for a look," Lyons said, groaning.

Lanno had already swerved to the right, heading off the freeway and onto an exit ramp with mere inches to spare.

"WHAT DO YOU HAVE?" Lyons asked, staring at the eight bodies lying in various macabre positions in the narrow, blood-covered alleyway. High-rise tenements lined the alley, blocking out the rising sun.

"And just who are you guys?" a stocky sergeant asked, turning to face them.

"They're okay," Lanno said, throwing the gearshift into park and chaining the steering wheel to the brake pedal before alighting from the van. "They're with me."

"And just who the hell are you?" the sergeant asked again, resting his gun hand on the exposed pistol butt of a holstered .357 Magnum. He was a big man, around six-four, with well over two hundred pounds of muscle on a big-boned frame. Six white letters emblazoned across his black name tag spelled out Weston. A two-inch scar ran horizontally across one cheek beneath his right eye. His mustache was black and bushy, reminding Schwarz of a walrus.

Lanno, like the three Able Team commandos, was clad in grubby border attire and hadn't shaved in several days. "INS," he answered, producing ID. "And they're with the government."

The El Paso police sergeant surveyed Lyons and the others critically. He still didn't like what he saw. They looked more like wetback *pollos*, he thought. "Ours or theirs?"

"Very funny," Lyons said, stepping forward another few feet into the sergeant's space. "Any witnesses? Suspect description? Direction of travel?" He glanced around, but despite the presence of over a dozen marked police units, there were no bystanders monitoring the commotion.

A cautious smile cracked the sergeant's grim features, and he tugged at his ear. "Oh, I got it now," he said. "You guys are FBI. Well, I sure as shit didn't call in no FBI glory boys, and I sure as shit am in charge of this here scene, let me tell you."

"We're not FBI," Blancanales said, stepping up beside Ironman. "And we're not here to take over your investigation, Sarge."

"We just happened to be working a case down south that might be related," Schwarz said, "and thought we'd compare MOs, see if there are any similarities involved."

The big patrol sergeant seemed to reconsider. He glanced at his wristwatch. "Why not?" he said, waving them under the yellow tape sealing off the alley. "Just don't touch anything, or I'll have your goddamn heads on a PD-blue platter."

"We're not rooks, Sarge," Lyons muttered as he started toward the nearest body. "Thanks."

"Rookies I can trust," the veteran cop muttered. "They're usually so paralyzed with fear of disturbing a crime scene that they don't touch shit. It's hot dog supercops I always got to worry about."

"He sure likes the word shit," Schwarz whispered to Blancanales as they brushed past the sergeant.

"I think he's so full of it that his green eyes just turned brown," Blancanales quipped.

"I heard that," the sergeant shot back without visually following their progress across the blood-smeared pavement, but he didn't sound sufficiently enraged to pursue the taunt.

The alleyway was narrow—roughly fifteen feet across—and paved with a combination of street asphalt and playground blacktop. To the left was a sprawling two-story adobe structure with two black granite spires. Assumption Church had been built on two cramped acres of land owned by the local Catholic archdiocese. A parochial grammar school and reception hall had been added in the past decade, effectively cutting in half a vast parking lot now protectively fenced in by chain link and sagging loops of decorative wrought iron. The place had more of a Gothic graveyard look than that of a church. To the right, apartment buildings rose four, five and six stories high. Lyons's eyes scanned balconies—only a few lights glowed dimly several floors up, and they were quickly being extinguished one at a time. Down the alley, at the foot of a gently sloping incline, sparse traffic passed on an intersecting public thoroughfare. The alleyway continued beyond that for several more blocks.

Lyons had already dropped to one knee beside the nearest corpse. The shadows of four uniformed El Paso patrolmen, standing nearby as they secured their side of the crime scene, fell across his face.

The body obviously belonged to a woman in her late twenties or early thirties. He could tell that much by her figure and complexion—what was left of it. She wore tight black leotards, torn at the calves, and low-cut tennis shoes, also black. Leotards and tennis. Obviously a *pollita*, although he doubted she'd crossed over the border recently. Her blouse was a tattered creamy color, with huge blood-laced holes where a half-dozen exit wounds had left shards of gaping gristle along the backbone, from shoulder blades to hips. The blouse was a good Rodeo Drive imitation. She had quickly become Americanized. Until tonight. Long dark brown hair, matted with twigs and debris, and already clotted with more blood, fanned across her back.

"What have we got, Carl?" Schwarz asked.

"Hispanic female, about twenty-eight, twenty-nine, I'd say," Lyons answered as he carefully took hold of the woman's shoulders, glancing back to see if Sergeant Weston was watching, then carefully lifted the corpse onto its side. Her blouse was open, the buttons torn down the middle by the fall or the hot lead or a combination of both. Her exposed breasts, full, firm and a fleshy peach color—in contrast to the streaks of dark red oozing forth between them—flapped first to the left, then the right as the dead-weight shifted in Lyons's hands. Blood suddenly gushed from two bullet holes directly over the heart, but the flow quickly abated as Ironman lowered her upper torso slightly to accommodate gravity and the ongoing processes of rigor mortis already setting in.

Purple dots marked the spot where additional splinters of lead had penetrated the heart itself. "Died instantly, probably before she hit the ground," Lyons said. "Less than half an hour ago." His thumbnail scratched at a black smear across the woman's cheek.

"Powder burns?" Schwarz asked.

"Good guess, Gadgets," Ironman said, nodding. "I'd say she was shot at point-blank range from less than five or six feet." While bracing the lifeless corpse with one hand, he gently probed one of the lower bullet holes that had caused her belly to begin swelling unnaturally.

"Think you ought to be doing that?" Blancanales asked, obviously nervous now as he glanced back at Weston again.

"You're probably right," Lyons said, grinning. "Coroners get upset over guys like me tampering with dead people before they get flatboarded to the morgue but, gosh—too late, already found what I was looking for." Smile stretching ear-to-ear now, he lifted his blood-smeared fingertips for Rosario's inspection. They held a misshapen slug of lead.

"Rifle round?" Schwarz asked, dropping to one knee beside Lyons.

"Most definitely."

"M-16?" Blancanales asked, swallowing loudly.

"Negative, *amigo*. AK to the max," Lyons said, holding the round up to the bright burst of flashing blue and red police lights that filled the alley.

"AK as in AK-47?"

"Roger that. She was stitched right up the middle at close range by somebody who enjoyed what he—or she—was doing. See?" He gestured toward the woman's face, which displayed no overt evidence of anguish or terror in the frozen features. "She died with her eyes open, but without realizing what was going down right in front of her, what was going to happen to her."

"You can't tell all that by the look on her face," Gadgets challenged. "No way. I was born at night, man, but not *last* night."

"The hell I can't," Lyons said, his smile fading. "I've been skidding up to crime scenes for a long, long time."

"Well, you ain't a cop anymore," Blancanales reminded him. "You're one of us now. Let's leave this to the El Paso PD and hope it turns out to be just a random—"

"Random liquor store robbery gone awry?" Lyons let out a demonic laugh as he held out his hands, palms up, defying either man to point out *any* kind of storefront business nearby. He moved to the next body like a tomcat inspecting dead rodents that had washed up out of the sewer after a storm. "Or a bungled kidnapping of Catholics, perhaps? I don't think so. This ain't your garden variety psycho shooting, Gadgets," he said, examining the body of a young man in his late teens who had been nearly decapitated by a burst of high-caliber rounds. "Hell, this ain't even your routine mass murder. Can't you see it? Don't you smell it?"

"See what?" Schwarz asked warily, uncertain what Lyons was getting at. "*Smell* what?"

"All I smell is spilt blood," Blancanales said, his nostrils wrinkling. "And I don't like it. It reminds me of..." But his voice trailed off as the wail of two mournful sirens announced the arrival of a couple of unmarked detectives' units.

"Exactly," Lyons said as if reading Blancanales's mind as his eyes gauged the investigators' shrill arrival. Dull blue Pontiac Satellites, both vintage 1976, rolled up to the scene from different directions at nearly the same time. A red spotlight glowed faintly from the corner of one of the windshields. A blue strobe pulsated on the other's dashboard. "You were going to say it reminds you of the war. Well, that's it exactly, Rosario," he confirmed, gently lying the dead man's body back against the moist blacktop. "This ain't no simple scum bag shooting in the big city. It's what's left of a one-sided war zone, man. An ambush. I'd lay you odds the whole *lot* of them were mowed down by automatic rifles. It's here, brothers...."

"What's here?" Sergeant Weston asked as he escorted the two El Paso investigators to the body lying at Ironman's feet.

"The war has come to Texas, gentlemen," Lyons said, rising, hands on hips and feet slightly apart in a defensive stance. "From Central America."

"And it appears that nobody's safe, Sarge," Blanca-nales added as he knelt beside a third corpse. It belonged to an older man in his late fifties. He was wearing the black suit and white collar of a Catholic priest.

8

No witnesses came forth at the slayground behind Assumption Church that morning. Investigators from three different agencies canvassed the neighborhood, asking questions, offering small city council-funded rewards for information—without any luck.

Investigators determined that over three hundred bullets had been fired in that narrow alleyway during a two-minute period. Five- and six-story-high apartment buildings rose around the Church. A low-income housing tenement towered ten stories directly behind the fifty-year-old adobe church. Someone had to have seen something.

Yet the residents of north El Paso remained cryptically quiet. It was almost as if a curse had been placed on the neighborhood—a taboo against talking. Nobody had seen anything. Nobody had heard a sound. There was nobody who was willing to come forth in public *or* private. But the crime scene itself finally provided much needed clues.

"Get a load of *this*!" a rotund detective clad in brown polyester pants and sport coat yelled. He was squatting beside the woman Lyons had been examining earlier. Apparently Ironman had missed something crucial on his initial inspection. From the dead female's mouth the balding investigator withdrew an olive-drab patch bearing the outline of a warp-winged eagle clutching a cluster of lightning bolts and battle-axes in both clenched talons. In the wicked-looking bird's beak was a tiny, half-severed human. Below the winged predator were three words: El Playon Brigade.

"El Salvador's secret police," the detective said, pushing drooping wire-rim glasses back up a long, sloping nose as his pudgy forefinger tapped the black eagle's beak. "At least that's what this emblem represented last time I read a bulletin from San Salvador's top cop. It's on his stationery, too."

"What?" Schwarz and Lyons asked, both drawing closer.

"You're kidding," Ironman said. "Tell me you're kidding, bud."

"Wish it were so," the investigator returned, dropping the patch onto the woman's bullet-riddled chest as he rose to his full height of five-eight and extended a meaty hand. "Nice to see you again, Carl, I think." His eyes surveyed the Able Team commando's dirty clothes. "Welcome to El Paso. *Despite* whatever it is that brings you here."

"Bad luck brings me here, Sickles. It always does. You know that."

"Yeah. Life's a bitch and then you—"

"One of my mottos."

"There it is," Sickles said simply.

Lyons picked up the patch and ran his own fingers over the three Spanish words. "El Playon Brigade?" he questioned as his eyebrows came together. "Any applicable translation?" he asked at large, his eyes wandering over the scene of slaughter, seeking something tangible to sink his teeth into.

"Unknown, pal," Sickles said.

Lyons's gaze shifted to Blancanales. "Rosario? What's it mean?"

"Never heard of it," Politician said. "I don't believe the first two words stand for anything special or significant. Nothing impressive. More like a place."

"A place?"

"A town or village or something."

Lyons slipped the blood-caked patch into his breast pocket.

"Hey!" Sickles yelled, his objection carrying little enthusiasm. "That's evidence, Carl."

"Temporarily misappropriated," Lyons answered, forcing a smile. "I'm sure there's plenty more where that came from." His eyes remained ice-cold, their depths a mysterious murky blue. "Seven other mouths to feed, that is—and El Playon Brigade willing to oblige them all, apparently."

"You two know each other?" Blancanales asked quizzically.

"We do indeed," the El Paso investigator said, shifting his stance.

"Yes," Lyons concurred, nodding without smiling. "From way back...."

But if Ironman's sad countenance seemed to indicate their old relationship was one that pained him, nothing could be further from the truth. The ex-LAPD policeman had a great deal of respect for Detective Sickles, first on a professional basis and, finally, through a one-on-one, off-duty experience.

Lyons first met the investigator when a serial killer case took him from the City of Angels to Santa Fe, Houston and then finally El Paso, where Sickles had personally tracked down, cornered and terminated the ruthless murderer after dedicating three weeks and nearly a hundred hours of gratis overtime to the case—his own time spent loitering on skid row and wandering the housing projects where it had been reported the suspect was seen on a number of recent occasions.

The city of El Paso would never have authorized so much overtime rounding up *any* out-of-town murderer, much less one who had yet to end the life of any of its citizens. But Sickles had a personal vendetta in this case.

Whether simply a stroke of bad luck, or destiny at its most just limits, the mass murderer had chosen the El Paso detective's niece—then attending college in East Los Angeles at Cal State—as his thirteenth victim.

Detective Second Grade Kelly K. Sickles—three hundred pounds and five-eight on his best days, a six-pack heavier when the job beat him down—gave his all in the search for mass murderer Pedro González. And Sickles prevailed, putting to rest forever the jokes, catcalls and snide remarks from younger, more handsome and physically fitter patrolmen gracing the uniformed ranks and aspiring to someday fill the shoes and possess the gold badge case of the pudgy investigator.

After attending the police academy, Sickles had quickly become aware that he didn't want to remain long in "the bag"—cop slang for uniformed duty. Two years attending bar fights and family disturbances had been quite enough, thank you. As soon as he was eligible, Sickles applied for the only investigator slot open—in the juvenile division. It was a much-shunned position, for the most part. Who wanted to waste time trying to steer delinquents away from petty thievery and gang rumbles when there was real crime fighting to be done from the front lines of black-and-white duty? But Sickles was smart. He saw it as a stepping-stone, and within two years had advanced to the burglary squad. Eventually, after bagging a notorious cat burglar who had been preying on some of El Paso's wealthier residents, Robbery/Homicide was emblazoned across the door to his office cubicle.

Following the three-mile rooftop chase and semihorrific shoot-out with Pedro González—in which Sickles fired off all the rounds of .45-caliber ammo in his possession before felling the vicious serial killer—the El Paso PD's chief of detectives no longer threatened to demote the beefy cop because of his weight problem. The top cop in southwest Texas figured that if Sickles could successfully pursue a man half his weight and ten years his junior over that great a distance—and not even strike a single innocent bystander with any of the hollowpoints he'd popped off that evening—he could hardly fault the man for a few dozen unauthorized pounds. Instead, the now-legendary investigator was instantly promoted.

It had taken twenty-one bullets to finally stop his target. Only four had actually struck González: three in the right cheek of the posterior, and the final hollowpoint in the left shoulder blade, exiting through the heart *after* giving the aorta a .45-caliber overhaul. After the shoot-out, Sickles took to carrying nearly a hundred extra rounds of ammunition with him at all times. When the department authorized it in the late eighties, he also began packing a newer 9 mm automatic instead of the tried-and-true Colt Mark IV. This switch enabled him to keep nearly twenty rounds in the magazine, ready for action. It had maybe a tenth as much firepower as the hoodlums haunting the El Paso underworld had, but it was better than next to nothing, which was the way he now felt about his old Colt .45. Sickles also spent more time practicing on the firing range after faring so poorly—shot for shot—out in the real world. For the first time in his police career he even earned an expert marksman's badge. Being a plainclothes investigator, though, he found few opportunities to wear it. Instead he framed a photo depicting himself in black SWAT coveralls posing on the firing range. Then he glued the marksmanship ribbon between the glossy eight-by-ten enlargement and a recent departmental certificate for bravery. The award plaque was one of the few decorations gracing the walls of his modest bachelor apartment in east El Paso.

Now Sickles stared down at the dead, half-naked Hispanic woman. His eyes shifted to the patch Lyons had just taken from his pocket and handed to Pol, then scanned the scene of carnage extending several yards down the narrow alleyway. "Any evidence kits en route?" he asked Weston.

"On the way," the police sergeant answered. "Radioed for the lab truck five minutes after I pulled up on this abortion. You want the mobile command post, too?"

Frowning, Sickles glanced over at Weston, unsure if he was trying to sound sarcastic. "It won't be necessary," he replied without emotion. Turning to Lyons, he asked, "What do you think about that patch, Carl?"

"Bullshit," Ironman said as he commandeered a patrolman's flashlight and began checking the other corpses. Similar patches had been placed in the mouths of every lifeless body left behind Assumption Church.

"Bullshit?" Sickles questioned, his eyes roaming the dark, shadowy balconies above.

"Something left here to throw us off course, to make us think the Salvadoran secret police have actually dispatched a death squad across international borders via Mexico."

"You don't accept that theory?" Sickles asked as he produced a pocket notebook and began scribbling down some preliminary observations. "It's been a long standing rumor for the past couple of years, you know."

"That the government of El Salvador would send assassins up here to silence outspoken refugees critical of their politicians and military back home?"

"Right-O."

"Well, I think the whole Central American refugee problem is nothing more than a propaganda ploy," Lyons said, speaking carefully, well aware he might hear snickers even among fellow law-enforcement types. But he heard nothing except a tense silence. And sirens in the distance.

"A super Commie plot, eh?" Sickles said, grinning.

"Something like that." Lyons's eyes narrowed threateningly.

After pausing a moment for dramatic effect, Sickles dropped to one knee to examine the dead woman's exit wounds before saying, "It just so happens I think you're right."

Schwarz responded first. "You do?"

"Exactly. The government of El Salvador is an ally of the United States, right?"

"That's what they tell me. *Despite* what the American news media disseminates from L.A. to New York."

Sickles cleared his throat before continuing. "Well, the way I see it, political refugees from East Bloc nations and the Middle East don't flee to the Soviet Union for safe haven, do they? Why should I believe that so-called political refugees from El Salvador would flee to the U.S.— especially if the U.S. is the benefactor and supporter of El Salvador."

"You've got a pretty damn good point there, Detective," Blancanales said, rubbing at the stubble on his chin in reflection. He was genuinely impressed with Sickles's rationalization.

"I think every refugee coming up through Central America to Mexico, and eventually the U.S., is nothing more than a pawn—or perhaps, dare I say it?—an agent of the Sanctuary Movement, conspiring, for propaganda purposes, to discredit the democratic regimes of their homelands," Sickles continued, his eyes rising again to inspect the countless balconies protruding above them.

"Well, some of those south of the border might argue with you about how democratic their governments actually—" Agent Lanno began.

But Blancanales's glare cut him off as he scanned the short Hispanic's features. "Lanno?" he questioned. "What kind of name is that, kid? It sure as hell ain't Mexican."

"My adoptive father was American," Lanno replied, lifting his chin slightly. "My biological parents were both killed in an earthquake back in the fifties in northern Mexico. My adoptive parents were missionaries with the Peace

Corps, working the border regions. They took me in when I was only a few months old. And I took their name. You got a problem with that, mister?''

If Lanno was expecting a compassionate response from Politician, he was sorely mistaken. "Peace Corps, huh?" Blancanales said, producing his most evil grin. "How'd you ever end up being a cop?"

"I ain't a cop," Lanno said, folding his arms across his chest. "I work for the Border Patrol."

Behind him, Zamora snickered. "Ain't *that* the truth," he said, laughing, a crook in his body at the midsection as he leaned his elbow on his holstered gun butt.

"Well, politics aside, these patches are all we've got to work with right now," Sickles said, holding one up to the flickering blue beams from the nearest patrol car. "I'll have the boys in Austin attempt a chemical lift of any prints, then have them run through the latents computer."

"You won't find any fingerprints," Lyons said. "I'd wager a week's pay the shooters all wore gloves."

Sickles was down on one knee again as the first shaft of sunlight pierced the early-morning fog and lanced down between two apartment buildings. And he was smiling. "Pay up," he told Lyons.

Cautiously he placed the eraser end of a pencil into one of the empty brass AK cartridges abandoned at the scene, then held the shell up to the light. "Mistake number one: they neglected to use brass catchers on their rifles," the investigator said. "Mistake number two: they were careless back at their base when they loaded up for this midnight mission."

Even from five feet away Lyons could see the partial print, highlighted by grimy oil, clinging to the side of the shiny brass cartridge.

Blancanales slung his CAR-15 assault rifle for the first time since arriving at the shooting scene. "Well, I'd say you obviously don't need us here anymore. Therefore, since we're due for a little shut-eye..."

"Thanks for the assist," Sickles told Lyons. "Pentagon been keeping *your* death squad busy, has it?" His eyes darted from Blancanales to Schwarz, then back to Ironman.

"You could say that," the ex-cop said, forcing a grin. "Been working a boiler room sting on the other side of the city."

"Heard about that," Sickles said.

"And it's brought in more dead fish than you can shake a pussycat at."

"Well, keep me posted. Maybe there's a connection."

"I'm positive there is. I just haven't been able to figure it out yet." Lyons turned to Lanno. "What do you say we take your van back down to the Border Patrol barracks and catch some sleep, Big L?"

"I wish you guys would quit calling it a barracks," Zamora said, loudly snapping the flap on his holster shut as he started back toward the vehicle. "It's more of a—"

Faint discharges in the distance silenced the agent. Immediately following the dozen or so sharp reports, an eerie quiet fell over the alley. Only the soft, almost subliminal grinding sound of several nearby emergency lights revolving in their turrets atop the roofs of squad cars could be heard.

"Was that what I think it was?" Lyons finally asked.

"Rifles," Lanno said as the far-off crackle resumed for a few seconds, then sputtered, faded, grew to a dull crescendo again and finally died out completely for the last time. "South of the border. Mexico," he whispered hopefully.

"Coming from south of the border?" Blancanales challenged. "You sure?"

Lanno's response was to hold up both hands and display crossed fingers.

"In El Paso we don't roll to shots fired in the night," Zamora said proudly.

"Unless they're fired close up and directly *at* you," Lanno countered.

"We wait for an official complaint...an official dispatch," Zamora continued. "Shit, otherwise we'd be running our butts ragged from dusk to dawn from one side of the city to the other, chasing wild geese."

"Wonder what *she's* looking at?" Blancanales said as he stared up at one of the dark balconies overhead.

A young, slender, Hispanic woman clad in a short, filmy nightgown that rode shapely hips and barely concealed a firm, upturned bosom was leaning against her balcony railing, gazing down at them with a blank face partially hidden in the shadows.

"What's she looking at? Well, you can have your choice," Sickles said, offering an answer for Politician. "Eight dead bodies, about a hundred flashing lights, a multitude of uniforms, or—"

"I prefer to think she's laying her dark, exotic eyes on what she considers to be God's gift to women," Gadgets Schwarz said. "Yours truly, gentlemen—Hunk, Incorporated."

Blancanales grinned. "*Three* hunks."

Lyons didn't smile, however. "Check out the cheekbones," he said.

"I'm checking out a set of legs that go on forever," Schwarz announced.

"Let's trot on up there and ask a few questions," Ironman suggested, his tone devoid of even the slightest hint of lust. "She's not your typical El Paso Mexican."

"I beg your pardon," Zamora said, feigning mild insult.

"No offense," Lyons said quickly. "But I've seen the telltale traits before. Down in Central America. Guatemala or Honduras."

"Honduras, my ass," Sickles snorted, then laughed.

"Okay," Lyons agreed, shrugging. "El Salvador."

"Lot of the women down there carry a unique beauty in their features," Blancanales said.

"Women in war zones *always* look good after a day humping across rice paddy berms, sidestepping leeches and kraits." Sickles sighed.

Taunted and teased in Vietnamese.... Sickles had been an MPI agent in Saigon twenty years earlier—when he was 120 pounds lighter and a *lot* younger. His older brother had been with CID—Criminal Investigations Division, the Army's version of a detective bureau. Tonight the similarities vaulted him right back to Vietnam's capital city, and all the sights, sounds and smells of the Pearl of the Orient rushed back to haunt him. Staring up at the woman, he heard VC on the rooftops...the pitter-patter of little feet, tightroping along the red-tiled rain gutters. And the words... The laughter that always swirled down from above, moments before a trash can filled with bricks was tossed at him and his partner.

"Yeah." Detective Kelly K. Sickles sighed loudly. "Women in war zones. Dey put da spell on ya, brotha, if'n ya don' watch out!"

"Whatever," Lyons said, shaking his head and exhaling. "Let's go."

A multitoned alert scrambler, issuing from the radio speakers of the dozens of patrol units blocking the alleyway, filled the early-morning air with a high-pitched yelp, freezing Able Team in its tracks.

"All units," a female dispatcher droned without excitement but in a firm, businesslike voice. "Vicinity Pierce and Copia Streets—shots fired. Possible automatic weapons involved. Multiple victims down in the street. Paramedics en route. Charlie-six, your call is Code-Three. Units to back, identify."

The radio network became a din of confused chatter as units across the city, preparing to make their way back to the HQ gas pumps for refueling, radioed in their call signs and present locations instead. "Have the paramedics hold off five or six blocks from the scene until our people arrive to assess the situation!" a sergeant directed in a no-nonsense voice.

"Ten-four, Sam-Seven."

Lyons locked eyes with Lanno. "Pierce and Copia?" he questioned.

"That's close to here," the border patrolman said as he made a break for the van. "About a mile or so southeast."

"Let's beat feet!" Ironman ordered, but Blancanales and Schwarz were already in the van, waiting for him.

THE U.S. BORDER PATROL van in which Able Team and two INS agents were riding barreled down McKelligon Canyon Road. Comanche Peak, rising nearly a mile high to their south, partially obscured the ascending sun as Zamora kept the speedometer riding fifty miles per hour, even through the curves.

A static-filled voice erupted from the radio mounted below the dashboard. Lyons caught the last few words of the transmission. "Border Patrol's got a unit en route also, Dispatch. Advise them of that vehicle description!"

Zamora grabbed the microphone with his gun hand while he steered with his left. "Thanks, Communications! I monitored the description. Confirm *no* plates visible."

"That's ten-four."

"Roger, thanks!"

"*What* description?" Lyons exploded. "*I* didn't hear any goddamn description."

"That's what you get for riding back in the chopper cabin as expendable cargo, mate!" Zamora quipped, beginning to sound like an insane RVN-stationed Aussie who'd commandeered an American gunship for an R and

R to Bangkok. "We're looking for a black mid-eighties Volvo sedan, tinted windows, no license plates. Got all that?"

"Where the hell did you learn to drive?" Blancanales asked, his knuckles white as he grasped the nearest handhold protruding from the vehicle's walls.

"Any complaints?" Zamora asked, grinning like a demon on a pizza run to hell and back.

"I was thinking of sending a letter of congratulations to your instructor. *If* you keep this crate on the road!"

"California Highway Patrol," Zamora said, beaming. "Class Three of 1985."

"What happened?" Blancanales asked.

"Got tired of being a traffic cop. Got assigned to South Bay. Got a bad attitude putting up with rich and arrogant brats."

"So you joined the Border Patrol."

"Got drafted," Zamora corrected, his smile fading.

"Huh?" Schwarz and Lyons both replied simultaneously.

"Forget it," Zamora said, shrugging.

"Private little joke," Lanno explained without shedding any further light on the comment.

"Oh," Gadgets moaned, his teeth rattling as they roared over a section of bad pavement.

"The least you could do is turn on your friggin' siren," Lyons recommended.

"Wish I could," Zamora answered as he swerved around a dog that had wandered out into the road in front of them. "Blew a fuse on the hot run from Saint Mikey's to Assumption."

"Shit," Blancanales muttered.

"You called?" Lanno said, glancing over his shoulder.

"Yes?" Zamora asked, glancing back as well, his ear-to-ear grin visible again.

Lyons closed his eyes tightly as a beat-up old truck, appearing out of nowhere along the side of the road, backed directly into their path half a block in front of them.

"Hold on to your gonads," Lanno announced, as if he'd been through the routine many times before. "Pucker factor's about to increase to warp ten."

And it just about did as the van made a hard right onto Alabama Street, missing the truck by inches.

"Whooooooeeee!" Schwarz cried out as he lost his grip on the handhold and bounced off the opposite wall.

Less than a minute later Zamora was tugging the steering wheel hard in the other direction. Out of a window Lyons saw that the street signs now read Pierce Avenue. The sun was in their eyes, still low along the horizon and straight through the windshield.

That didn't slow Zamora in the least. "Copia Street coming up next," he announced by stomping the gas pedal to the floor. "In about zero-five."

"Is that five seconds or five min—" Gadgets began to ask, but his query was cut short as Zamora slammed on the brakes, bringing the van into a sideways skid down the middle of Pierce Avenue.

"What the fu—" Lyons yelled, latching on to a loose rifle as it bounced around in the back of the van.

"There they are!" Zamora cried, pointing a rigid forefinger at a black Volvo mid-eighties headed directly toward them.

The Volvo fishtailed as its driver attempted to avoid crashing into the van head-on. His left rear fender struck the van's front bumper as both vehicles met, bounced off each other and skidded away in opposite directions.

The Border Patrol van ground to a halt—its wheel well smashed into a front tire—and the Volvo's driver expertly brought his car into a counterclockwise spin while it was still moving in reverse. "We're dealing with fucking pros!" Lyons observed as they watched the black four-door slide all the way around until it was heading forward again, sheer momentum propelling it away from the bewildered lawmen.

"Damn it!" Blancanales cried as he jumped from the van and, hands on hips, watched the Volvo disappear beyond a rising cloud of dust.

Lanno slid up beside him, assault rifle against his shoulder, but Politician knocked the barrel skyward before the border patrolman could pop off the first round.

"Why the hell'd you do that?" Lanno yelled.

"PC," Blancanales said. "Our PC was weak, kid. Plus, there's too much innocent traffic down the road, and you didn't have a clear enough shot."

"PC? What the hell are you talking about—PC!"

"Probable cause," Blancanales explained calmly. "Cops can no longer shoot fleeing felons, you know. Not even in Texas. Besides, we're not even sure they were our bad guys."

"*What?*" Lanno demanded.

"All we have right now, technically, is a hit-and-run traffic accident."

"You've got to be shittin' me!" Lanno growled, eyes bulging incredulously.

"I wouldn't shit you, kid. You're my favorite turd," Pol responded calmly.

"Damn!" Lanno pounded his own thigh in frustration and circled the Able Team commando, dancing a tight madman's jig around Blancanales.

The ex-black beret glanced back at the racket Lyons was making as he and Zamora worked frantically with a crowbar to pry the dented fender away from the tire.

"Well, hell!" a dejected Lanno said, ramming the butt of his rifle against the earth. Blancanales winced, but the weapon didn't discharge.

"What's wrong?" Schwarz asked, rushing up between them as four El Paso police cars raced past in rapid succession, lights and sirens in operation. He watched them vanish in the direction the Volvo had taken, then locked eyes with Rosario. "Why didn't you guys blow those suckers away, Pol?"

"See! *See!*" Lanno rose up on his toes, nose to nose with Blancanales. "Even your own buddy agrees with me!" he sputtered. Lanno's jig became an I-told-you-so waltz as he rocked back precariously on his heels. Politician couldn't resist, and gently pushed him off balance.

Quickly recovering, Lanno continued the verbal attack. "Hell, I thought you guys were supposed to be some hotshot super-elite commandos or something!"

Blancanales shook his head in resignation. "Do I have to explain it to *everybody*?"

"Let's go!" Lyons said, throwing the crowbar into the back of the van as Zamora slid behind the steering wheel and forced the gearshift into drive.

After Blancanales and the others had piled in, Zamora acknowledged the dispatcher, then announced, "They've got the vehicle at Arroyo Lake, a couple of miles west of here, off Rim Road."

"Any suspects in custody?"

"Doesn't sound like it."

"Wham, bam, thank you ma'am," Gadgets muttered.

Lyons glanced over at him. "Huh?"

"Screwed again."

9

Flesh peeling away from his face as the fireball engulfed his entire body, Rosario Blancanales sank back against the bed's headboard, naked and defenseless. Billowing plumes of black smoke from the dragon's flaring jaws choked and gagged him. The monstrous winged serpent was throwing its shoulders against the narrow doorway, trying frantically to force apart the frame to break into the room—to get at Rosario—but the doorframe, splintered and smoldering, continued to hold. The dragon was huge, its head the size of a Volkswagen. Its eyes sparkled like green diamonds as streams of silver smoke poured from flaring nostrils and another fireball burst forth through giant, gleaming teeth. "Coming to get you, Rosario!" The dragon had a woman's voice with an exotic, singsong tone common to the Orient. "Coming to get you tonight, Rosario!" And, lunging again, the fire-breathing dragon finally made it through the doorway. Splinters of wood showered onto the bed. As if by magic, an M-60 machine gun appeared in Rosario's hands, but when he pulled the trigger, the heavy weapon's long belt of bullets became a writhing, hissing cobra. When the golden snake sank its fangs into his cheek the scream that left the young soldier's scorched throat was a collective cry from every brother warrior who had ever died in his arms....

"Yo! Politician! Wake the hell up!"

Blancanales's eyes popped open as lights in the hotel room flashed on. He calmly scanned his surroundings: there was no dragon hunting him. No fire. No broken-down door. Only Gadgets Schwarz shaking his wrist, and Carl Lyons reaching for the telephone. Outside, sirens wailed as two police units raced past in the rain-slick street below. The screams in his nightmare had been the electronic wail of the El Paso PD squad cars.

"You were having a bad dream or something," Schwarz said.

"Or something," Blancanales agreed as his ears accepted, categorized and identified the ringing phone for the first time.

"Well, you don't seem too disturbed by it now," Gadgets said, shaking his head.

"Yeah..." Rosario said softly, rising from the bed. Like his two fellow commandos, he still wore his trousers and boots. Dropping into the push-up position, he began knocking them out. "One drill sergeant. Two drill sergeant..."

Yeah...not disturbed...calm now... The dragon that had followed him home from Vietnam still raised its ugly head now and then, but Blancanales no longer feared it. The dreams made no sense whatsoever. A goddamn fire-breathing dragon trying to break down his bedroom door. So what? The oversize lizard had never actually devoured him. The part about the M-60 becoming a king cobra was irritating as hell, though, and he had yet to figure *that* out—even after all these years of self-hypnosis and personal reflection.

But the dragon had never devoured him.

When them Gila monsters clamp onto you, kiss it goodbye, the border patrolmen's voices, out there in the pitch-dark overlooking Canine Canyon, returned to taunt him. *They're lazy and slow, but once they clamp onto you, they never let go! They just kinda grind away at the flesh, slowly*

*chewing...injecting poison with each bite. Just about takes
major surgery to get 'em off. Decapitation. It's the only
remedy....*

There had been a time, a few years back, when he had
been able to tell that he was dreaming—had actually been
able to gain control of the nightmare, slay the dragon. But
lately his weapons were jamming or turning into snakes or
useless punji sticks or even brittle bones of dead Vietnamese ancestors he didn't even have. And that, too, was most
irritating, for Rosario had always been proud of his Mexican heritage. But Blancanales was convinced he'd soon gain
the upper hand on the problem. Again. It was only a matter of time.

"Yeah, Chief..." Lyons was saying. "You got it, boss.
On our way. Right. Pronto." After hanging up the phone,
Ironman glanced at his two co-workers. "Man, is *he* on the
warpath."

"The Chief's in town?" Schwarz asked, his eyes light-
ing up.

"Yep," Lyons confirmed as he rose from his own bed
and began gathering up his gear. "He's waiting for us over
at El Paso police headquarters, and he wants us over there
yesterday!"

"I take it he got wind of the carnage that went down behind Assumption Church."

"That he did," Lyons said, nodding. "I phoned him after we set up camp this morning," he added, gesturing to
their surroundings—a cramped single-bed motel room that
management had agreed to supplement with two additional cots.

Able Team had been staying at the Border Patrol barracks all week but, as they were in dire need of three or four
hours of uninterrupted sleep, and the main INS barracks
was a whirlwind of activity during the day shift, they opted
for a low-profile motel on the southern edge of town.

"I'll fire up the chariot," Blancanales said, indicating the olive-drab Ford Bronco sitting outside. It had been assigned to them by Patterson.

"Good idea," Lyons said, producing a tight grin. "It'll give you something to do to keep your mind off what the Chief's got in store for us for letting the bad guys get away twice in twenty-four hours."

Blancanales's tentative smile faded instantly. Frowning, he stalked out of the motel room and kicked one of the Bronco's front tires.

A BIG MAN SAT alone in the empty police briefing room at El Paso police headquarters. As he studied a thick stack of documents, one hand absently scratched at a thick mane of hair while the other clamped his trademark unlit cigar between index and middle finger.

"Morning, Chief!" Gadgets Schwarz said, beaming as he led Able Team through the doorway of the cavernous room.

Silently growling, the bearlike man, seated with his back to an unpainted cinder-block wall, glanced up from the paperwork. Frown deepening, his eyes dropped back to the reports. He said nothing.

"Oh-oh," Blancanales whispered to Lyons as he feigned a nervous swallow.

Hal Brognola was Stony Man's chief of operations and liaison with the White House, Washington bureaucracy and various intelligence agencies and organizations based in the capital. He was older than most of the men who worked under him, and supervising responsibilities had tacked a decade or so of additional years to his appearance. His hand dropped, picked up a pen and began scribbling notes in his own indecipherable brand of shorthand as the fingers holding the Honduran cigar motioned the men up to the desk.

Brognola was a former specialist with the Justice Department in the area of covert operations, where he had served for many years before joining Stony Man Farm and taking the reins of the crime fighting trio known as Able Team. "You clowns haven't been doing so well on the target range," he said, finally glancing up again.

"And this ain't been your routine antiterrorist type of operation, either, Chief," Lyons returned, walking all the way up to Brognola's desk and leaning on its edge, lowering his nose to within inches of the big man's.

Brognola's gaze dropped to Ironman's scarred knuckles, shifted to lock eyes with the ex-policeman, then fixed on the fists again. Smiling, Lyons rose to his full height once more and backed off.

"Seriously, Chief," Blancanales said, coming to his colleague's rescue. "You sent us out here to help the locals catch some *banditos* on the border and keep an eye open for weekend terrorists of the Latin persuasion. Well, we bagged some bad guys who were preying on *pollos*, but the so-called terrorists must have made it through the checkpoint, 'cause we sure as hell didn't intercept them. So you can write off Los Angeles, I guess."

"No big loss," Brognola growled halfheartedly.

"That's the spirit!" Lyons said, chuckling.

"Then what happens?" Blancanales continued. "We accommodate the INS by backing up their boys on some shots-fired calls, and find ourselves in the middle of the Sanctuary Movement fiasco and a mass murder allegedly perpetrated by some death squad from Central America."

Brognola leaned back in his chair and plucked a black shoulder patch from his breast pocket. "El Salvador," he said, holding it up for their inspection. Still caked with blood, it was identical to the one Lyons had removed from the female corpse behind Assumption Church.

"How'd you get hold of that?" Blancanales demanded.

"He came by this morning," Lyons explained matter-of-factly. "While you two sleeping beauties were snoring up a storm. I briefed him and showed him the patch."

"And you didn't wake us?" Schwarz asked.

"He told me to let you bozos snooze a while longer. Said you deserved it."

"See, I've got a heart after all," Brognola said, grinning for the first time since their arrival.

"Three hours' worth of sleep," Blancanales said, frowning as he checked his watch. "Big deal."

Schwarz pointed at the Spanish words embroidered beneath the patch's mean-looking black eagle. "Any idea what it means, Chief?"

"Of course," Brognola said before chomping on his cigar. "That's why I'm the Chief. Somebody's got to have all the answers so we can get this show on the road."

Lyons glanced over at the access doors as a shapely policewoman with long red hair and a short blue skirt glided over to a bulletin board and began pinning departmental hot sheets to the wall.

"Sorry for the interruption," she said from forty feet away. "Don't mind me."

Four sets of eyes monitored the rise of her hemline to a point midway up firm thighs as she struggled to pin the reports to the only blank space on the cluttered board.

"If that's an example of El Paso's finest," Schwarz whispered to Lyons, "then gimme a recruit application, slick!"

"Uh-hum," Brognola said, clearing his throat. "Eyes forward," he commanded, tapping the patch with his cigar. "El Playon Brigade," he began without any trace of emotion, sympathetic or unfavorable. The Chief sounded totally neutral, in fact. "Affectionate title given to one of El Salvador's so-called death squads."

"That's confirmed?" Lyons asked.

"Confirmed," Brognola said, nodding, his eyes drifting back toward the bulletin board for only an instant.

"Eyes forward," Schwarz chided.

"There's a lava bed twelve miles north of San Salvador, the country's capital," Brognola explained. "Near an old, extinct volcano. It's called El Playon, and has been a favorite dumping ground for bodies since the civil war began down there ten years ago. Mainly bodies assassinated by alleged right-wing death squads—and I emphasize the word *alleged*. Can't believe everything the American news media tells you, right?"

"Ain't *that* the truth," Blancanales muttered under his breath.

"Anyway," Brognola continued, "the El Playon Brigade, according to my contacts within the San Salvador police, is an extremist faction of the National Republican Alliance, better known as ARENA and often linked to death squad activity blamed on the right."

"But that eagle there," Lyons said, pointing to the patch as Blancanales and Schwarz glanced over their shoulders to steal peeks at the policewoman, "is the insignia of the El Salvador secret police."

"Unofficial insignia," Brognola said. "One of many. But I've never seen the two combined: the eagle and the words El Playon Brigade. This is something new, which tends to make me incredibly suspicious, to put it mildly."

"You mean someone might be committing these murders and trying to lay the blame on the authorities down in El Salvador?" Lyons asked.

"It's entirely possible."

"They're pretty wild down there," Blancanales said. "The cops in San Salvador even make our brand of jungle justice pale in comparison to their methods."

"We don't torture our prisoners," Lyons snarled.

"There have been atrocities committed by both sides down there," Brognola commented stonily as the four men all turned to watch the policewoman leave the room with an arousing sway of hips.

"*My* partners in the LAPD never looked like that," Lyons complained after she was out of earshot. "At least none that I remember."

"She was wearing a red, white and blue ribbon over her badge," Brognola commented respectfully, and all the wolf leers vanished. "I take it none of you noticed *that*."

"Medal of Valor?" Lyons asked, glancing out the door again, but the female officer was long gone.

"Yep." The Medal of Valor was the highest award for bravery given in law enforcement. It came in different shapes, sizes and colors, but demanded the same level of intense respect across the country.

Brognola surveyed the faces of his men, knowing they would view the policewoman in a different light if they saw her again. Their eyes would probably fall to her gun belt instead of her hips, curious to see what kind of service weapon she preferred to pack, rather than determine her brand of panty hose. "Back to business," the Chief said with obvious regret.

"So what's our next move?" Gadgets asked, sounding anxious to get back out on the street.

Brognola produced a small remote control device, aimed it at the light switch on the opposite side of the room and pressed a button. "First," he said as the lights dimmed, "some background." Overhead and slightly behind Brognola, a slide screen dropped from the ceiling.

A projector sitting on a table below the bulletin board popped on with a bright flash, and a map of Central America appeared in the center of the eight-by-ten-foot screen.

"The civil war in El Salvador, as I said, has been going on for ten years," Brognola began, leaving the slide in place long enough to remind Lyons and the others that the country in question was south of Mexico and immediately outh of Guatemala and Honduras—two countries with which it shared its northern border. The Pacific Ocean radled the country along the south. "The government's rimary enemy down there is the leftist Faribundo Marti National Liberation Front...." Faces of guerrilla leaders, with their names stenciled beneath the file photos, began lashing across the screen.

"Recently guerrilla violence has extended from the ountryside into the urban areas—the cities. Car bombs ave been introduced. Assassinations of mayors in the rovinces surrounding the capital are commonplace. The J.S. government has poured nearly three billion dollars nto El Salvador, hoping to defeat the Communists by uilding up the Salvadoran military and supporting the resident.

"But the rebels appear to be growing stronger. Bolstering their full-time soldiers, which number about six thousand, is a broad network of part-time militia, which total over forty thousand. Weekend warriors, if you will. Their official role is to gather intelligence, carry messages, provide logistical support—even carry out propaganda and abotage. But make no mistake, they're fighters. Their hit-and-run surprise attacks have been very successful against he government's troops.

"The FMLN has basically given up on a military victory n El Salvador. Instead, they're hoping for a popular prising. Not much chance of that, though, so they've gone o far as to take part in elections, hoping to defeat the system politically." Brognola flipped a switch and the lights ame back on. The projector shut off and the screen rose.

"As I was saying, the Communists have given up on direct military action. Their weekend warriors are an important catalyst in this popular uprising scenario—working as a countryside liaison between the hard-core rebels and the ocal civilian sympathizers: *massas*.

"The Salvadorans call the weekend warrior *guerrilleros milicianos*. Their main support network comes from the People's Revolutionary Army, largest of the five groups in the Faribundo Marti."

A rustle of papers near the doorway attracted the men's attention, and all eyes turned toward the bulletin board. They were disappointed to find a grizzled, old, barrel-chested sergeant in his late fifties hanging mug shots and an FBI wanted poster this time.

"The chief of army operations down there recently told me that the militia is trained to murder in cold blood," Brognola continued. "They're mostly young idealogues from the universities, motivated by a need for cheap thrills and frustration over their country's faltering economy, where unemployment and inflation are both forty percent each and the country's per capita income is nearly thirty-nine percent lower than it was when the civil war started. They're vigorously protected by the Catholic Church...."

"Thus a motive for El Playon to go after the priests," concluded Blancanales.

"Right. There's little love lost between the Church and the El Salvadoran military."

"On whose scoreboard does the body count from Assumption Church go—the Salvadoran army, the right-wing death squads or the left wing FMLN?" Blancanales asked sarcastically.

"That's what you're here to find out," Brognola finally revealed. "No more border bandit stakeouts. And forget about terrorists with suitcase nukes sneaking around the INS checkpoints. The intel fizzled from day one. You give me the head of the man responsible for passing out these patches," he said, holding up the El Playon Brigade emblem, "and I'll be content for a change."

"Until the next big threat to democracy claws at that big body count scoreboard in the sky," Lyons muttered.

"So El Playon Brigade, or whoever they may really be," Politician interjected, "has compiled a death list, with the priests of the Sanctuary Movement at the very top."

"Something like that," Brognola said, nodding tentatively. "Don't forget there's a very real possibility that this death squad crap is purely that—bullshit."

"Imitators," Gadgets said, rubbing his chin. "Copycat killers."

"In a manner of speaking."

As Lyons listened to the discussion, his eyes locked onto a newspaper clipping someone had tacked to the wall. It showed a photo of armed security guards monitoring voting in Santa Ana, California, during the latest American presidential election. They had been hired by a politician to make sure no illegal aliens, trained in voter fraud and bussed to the polling places by left-wing agitators, were successful in shifting tide in favor of the Democratic side. The patrolman who had gone to the trouble of cutting out the article had scribbled across the grainy black-and-white photo, in red magic marker, "Shoot first and ask questions later! Bomb the Border!" Only in Southern California, Lyons thought.

Hal Brognola held up his own newspaper. It was a folded copy of the *El Paso Morning Star*. A front page headline proclaimed that Central American death squads had instigated a massacre of priests and undocumented workers in broad daylight behind Assumption Church. "I was hoping to avoid this," he said, slowly turning the paper until all three men had read the headline. "But we've never had an easy go of it, and I didn't expect fate to go easy on us now. Did any of you?"

No one answered.

From a thick file folder he next produced several eight-by-ten glossies of the Volvo sedan abandoned at the bottom of Arroyo Lake. "Tracks left at the scene indicated the lowlifes concealed three dirt bikes in the bushes near where they dumped the car. The pursuing officers lost them when they reached pavement on the west side of the park. It wasn't a total loss, however. A lone latent was raised off the car's gas cap—the only place they forgot to dust off their fingerprints. It matches the one taken off the empty shell casing found at the homicide scene behind Assumption Church.''

"Great!" Lyons said as he got to his feet.

Brognola anticipated his next question. "No NCIC identification yet," he said. "And no matchup through the FBI, either. But we're still working on it."

"And those three undocumented workers who survived the ambush at Pierce and Copia?" Blancanales asked.

"DOA at El Paso General Hospital's emergency room," Brognola advised them. "As you know, the other five illegals who were riding in the back of the truck with them died at the scene of multiple gunshot wounds."

"I doubt they were simple illegal farm workers," Lyons said, his eyes narrowing slightly. "I'd wager that if you did a brief background on them—"

"Already did," the big Fed said, nodding. "They were all Salvadorans—political activists back home. They died carrying propaganda leaflets printed in a back room of the rectory at Saint Michael's Church. Father Felipe had a regular underground printing press operation going on there."

"The shooters didn't have time to stuff their victims' mouths with El Playon Brigade patches," Gadgets said.

"True. But they threw a handful into the street at the shooting scene before fleeing at the approach of sirens. A couple of El Paso units were only a few blocks away."

"What about the Volvo? Anything left in—"

"Picked clean," Brognola answered, shaking his head. "Only thing they left behind was that one careless fingerprint."

"What about those two twirps calling themselves Francis and Cecilia?" Schwarz asked.

"They've clammed up tight."

"What about the two priests, Franco and Felipe?" Lyons cut in impatiently.

"They've got themselves a lawyer, who's refusing to let them talk to us. For now. It's only a matter of time."

"Which we don't have much of," Blancanales argued.

"Right," Brognola said, leading them toward the door. "The White House is afraid innocent American civilians may eventually wind up in the cross fire if this death squad business continues. Able Team is to locate, isolate and capture the group of assassins as soon as possible—and bring them in for questioning. *Alive*, if possible."

"That's a tall order," Lyons grumbled. "These bastards have an endless supply of guns and they like using them."

"Just give it your best shot, Carl."

"That's what we've been trying to do, Chief," Schwarz argued as they passed by a small squad room occupied by five or six detectives.

"Well, you'll just have to do better, Gadgets, or you're going to be assembling toilet bowls in Okinawa, son."

Brognola paused in the doorway. Two of the investigators were "reviewing" a confiscated porno video. The other three were watching a separate TV console, airing a debate in Congress. It was obviously a cable station.

One of Brognola's favorite congressmen was lambasting the speaker of the House. "I love that guy!" he said, laughing and waving a fist. "Give 'em hell, Bob!"

Outside, Schwarz suggested to Brognola that he join them on this mission. "Come along for the ride! See first-hand how we operate in the field."

"I've witnessed your battlefield antics on past occasions, Gadgets. It's safer up there," he said, pointing to an idling helicopter sitting on the police department's rooftop helipad, its fifty-foot blades twirling sluggishly. A pilot in

SWAT coveralls, pistol belt and black shades was standing by, a bored expression creasing his dark, weathered features.

"Eye in the sky, eh?" Lyons asked. "Gonna watch over us from on high, Chief?"

"Hardly," Brognola said, chomping down on his ever-present cigar. "I'm en route to the airport at Fort Bliss. Grimaldi and Cowboy Kissinger are waiting there for me with the C-12. We're taking a trip."

"Back to D.C.?"

"Nope," Brognola said, treating them to a casual half salute. "El Salvador."

10

After the briefing with Brognola at El Paso police headquarters, Able Team returned to the dilapidated apartment buildings overlooking the alley behind Assumption
Church. It was easy for both Lyons and Blancanales to spot
the balcony on which the attractive Hispanic woman had
been standing that morning at predawn: two crossed flags
from Panama hung from banners attached to the railing.

As Gadgets counted the stories, Ironman said, "Fifth
floor."

"Let's do it then," Blancanales said, starting for the
stairwell. There was no elevator.

Her door creaked open as they approached. "I knew you
would be back," she told them.

The woman, whose name was Ann-Marie, spoke fluent
English with only a slight accent. Lyons guessed her to be
no older than thirty. It was hard to tell. The skimpy negligee she had been wearing only hours before was nowhere to
be seen. Instead, she wore a modest white sweater and knee-
length skirt that accented her dark, teak-colored flesh. The
sweater was tight, focusing attention on the gentle sway of
full breasts. It was hard for Lyons and his partners not to
stare.

An infant lay sleeping silently in a crib against one wall
of the modest one-room apartment. Blue and purple birds,
fashioned from crepe streamers, hung suspended from the

ceiling directly over the crib. They twirled lazily as a draft moved through the drab room.

She didn't ask for their credentials. The men of Able Team volunteered no information as to what organization they belonged to. "I am a soldier's widow," she told them. "My husband worked with the American DEA, eradicating narcotics fields in the Panamanian jungle. His helicopter was shot down seven months ago."

"We're sorry," Blancanales said, lowering his eyes with sincerity.

"Blackhawks," she whispered, pointing to a dime store poster hanging on one wall, the only decoration in the room besides the birds.

"What?" Lyons asked, an image of the El Salvadoran secret police patch coming to life before his mind's eye.

"He flew Blackhawk helicopters. My brother was with him. Now both are dead. My girlfriend's father, too. It was a bad day in Panama City seven months ago."

"Yes," Blancanales said, nodding.

"Now my government gives me a pension. Your government gives me permission to live in this housing project. We couldn't stay in Panama. The drug lords would have found us. My son's body would have been fed to alligators. Mine would have been gang-raped and dumped in the Soto River...."

Schwarz inwardly shuddered as he envisioned the scene. He wandered over to a wall cabinet and noticed a small display case beneath framed photos of a soldier. He thought he recognized the uniform of Panama's army.

"May I?" he asked, indicating the glass-covered case. Inside, some sort of black stone sparkled back at him.

"Yes, of course," the woman answered, moving in lithe silence across the room to assist him. "It was my husband's. A ceremonial dagger from deep in the heart of some jungle in Mexico," she continued as she removed the ten-inch obsidian blade and held it out for all of them to see.

"Amazing," Gadgets commented, running his finger along the edge, which was sharp as a glass splinter. "It must be a thousand years old."

"Five hundred," the woman corrected him politely. "My husband told me it was stolen from an ancient Aztec temple, where the chieftains used it in sacrificial ceremonies."

"Pigs and goats?" Blancanales asked.

"Aztec virgins," she said, forcing a smile as Rosario swallowed loudly. "Many collectors have offered to buy it, but it is the only thing of value my husband left us, and I keep the thing in honor of his memory. We have no savings."

Gadgets handed the dagger back to the woman, and she respectfully placed it back in the display case. Blancanales winced as a cockroach dropped from the ceiling into the baby's crib. For some reason he thought of Saigon.

"About last night," Lyons said, walking over to the balcony, unfazed. He stepped outside and stared down at the shooting scene. "Please tell us what you saw."

"I saw very little. I heard many shots. A machine gun. Not like the kind used in Panama. They were brown wooden ones, with long, curving clips—banana clips."

"AK-47s."

"Yes," she said, nodding, her dark round eyes locking onto his in an odd, almost seductive manner. "AK-47s. My husband, Emilio, was a gun nut. He told me everything about American, Chinese, Mexican weapons. I truly believed he would die at the hands of a gunman. Instead, he dies in a helicopter crash."

"Mechanical failure?" Gadgets asked.

"It was shot down," she said matter-of-factly. "By a rocket-launched grenade."

"Oh . . ." Schwarz turned away and busied himself with a pitcher of water as she followed Lyons out onto the balcony.

"I was in bed," the woman continued.

Lyons recalled the image she'd presented in the early morning, standing on the balcony in the skimpy negligee.

"I heard the shots, but that is nothing new. We have many gangs here. Too many. But then the shooting didn't stop after a burst or two, as it always does. The shooting continued, and I heard a woman scream. Then I realized I wasn't dreaming. My ears began to hurt—even this high up . . . five floors. That was when I saw the priest. They were very cruel to him. . . ."

"Cruel?" Schwarz asked.

"Yes . . . very mean. They shot him in the knees, then they shot him in the belly. Many, many bullets—three men firing them. But the priest refused to die. He remained alive, on his side, eyes open wide—I could see his eyes way up here. His mouth was open, his hands up, raised toward the men with guns, pleading."

"What did they do?" Blancanales asked.

"They calmly reloaded their rifles and finished him off. A banana clip in the face. I wanted to throw up. Instead, I grabbed my rosary and called 911. I couldn't speak. I was terrified, but it was like magic. The woman on the other end . . . I could hear her talking. *She* could hear the gunshots over the phone. Somehow she knew my address—I heard her giving it to someone else. The police got here very fast. *You* got here very fast." Her eyes narrowed for the first time. They seemed laced with mild suspicion. "Who *are* you?" she asked.

"Friends of the police," Lyons said softly.

A wry smile crept across the woman's somber features. "I know who you are now," she said, leveling a rigid forefinger at Ironman. "You are the *secret* police."

Lyons continued to stare down at the lab technicians' chalk marks crisscrossing the murder scene below. Here and here an expended flashbulb from the old-fashioned police cameras glistened back at him. "Which way did they flee?" he asked Ann-Marie.

"Down the alley," she said, pointing toward the west. "There were four of them."

"Americans?" Schwarz questioned, taking a wild shot.

"Chicanos. Mexicans. They got into a car and sped away. I think a woman was driving."

"What kind of car?" Blancanales asked.

A streak of worry creased her features. "I don't know cars well," Ann-Marie admitted. "A small car."

"A Volvo?" Blancanales asked, although he didn't want to plant images in her head.

"Maybe..."

"What color was it?" Lyons asked, leaving the balcony and wandering over toward the kitchen table. His eyes nonchalantly scanned a cluster of mail.

"Black. All black, with the windows black, too." Her smile began to grow.

"Tinted?"

"Yes," she said, nodding her head enthusiastically. "A new word for today—is that what you call it? Tinted."

Lyons made a mental note that the envelopes all bore Panamanian stamps and red and blue air mail stripes along the edges. "Do you have any plans to leave here?" he asked.

"No," she answered quickly, no hint of dishonesty in her eyes or movements. "We...my son and I have nowhere else to go."

Blancanales handed her a business card with nothing but a toll-free phone number on it. "If anything happens or comes up," he told her, "call this number. The person you speak to will get in touch with us, and we'll contact you immediately, okay?"

"Yes...okay." A look of despair clouded Ann-Marie'
eyes as it became evident that these three confident me
were now about to leave her. "Some iced tea?" she asked
rushing to the tiny portable refrigerator. "Some sof
drinks? I'm afraid I don't have any beer, or I would—"

"We have to be going," Blancanales said, laying his hand
gently on her shoulder. "But thank you." Lyons and
Schwarz had already started out the door.

"There is one thing I just remembered!" she blurted out
head reeling now, mind racing to think of some way to keep
them just a few minutes more. "One other thing abou
them."

"What is it?" Rosario asked, taking her hand. H
glanced down at her fingers and noticed she was tremblin
with fear.

In the street below the jingling bells of an ice-cream ven
dor, patrolling the neighborhood for customers, drifted u
to reach their ears. "I remember seeing one of them be
fore," Ann-Marie said. "A week ago...maybe two. H
worked at the ice-cream parlor down the street, wher
Alabama and Pierce meet. Yes, the ice-cream parlor."

"Okay, We'll check it out," Blancanales told her.

"He was young," Ann-Marie added, biting into he
lower lip as the untruth escalated into a full-fledged fabri
cation. "Maybe twenty-four, twenty-five...with lon
brown hair over his shoulders, and many rings. He wor
rings on almost all his fingers, and he wore a red T-shirt...a
red Rambo T-shirt...and he also had a ring in his ear."

"Okay," Lyons said, giving her a tired wave. "We'l
check it out. Thanks."

"And thank you," Ann-Marie said, rushing over to th
door and taking Ironman's hands in hers. "Thank you fo
coming to check on me."

Lyons pulled away gently as Blancanales moved closer to
the woman. "Don't lose the card," he said, staring into the

epths of her unblinking eyes. "My name is Rosario. Remember it."

"Yes...Rosario," Ann-Marie said, nodding gratefully
s she stared back. "I will remember it."

HEY DIDN'T FIND an ice-cream parlor at the corner of
Pierce and Alabama Streets. But a block to the east, a
lender Hispanic with long hair, wearing a red T-shirt and
ons of costume jewelry had set up a vendor's wagon in an
lleyway. He was selling ice cream to all the little girls and
boys walking by.

"Don't lose the card," Lyons mimicked Blancanales as
hey sat in the back of their Border Patrol Bronco. "My
name's Rosario. Remember it."

"The widows of the world aren't even safe from Don
Juan here," Gadgets joined in.

"Hey!" Blancanales said, raising his hands defensively.
"What can I say, *amigos*? The woman looked like she
needed a shoulder to cry on."

"What's he doing now?" Schwarz asked, changing the
subject as he reached for the folding binoculars Lyons was
looking through. Ironman refused to surrender them.

"Still selling little plastic bags instead of ice cream,"
Lyons observed casually.

"Think it's dope?" Gadgets asked almost innocently
enough to crack a laugh from Blancanales.

"No, it's Kool-Aid. Of course it's dope. What did you
think?"

"Well, is he wearing a goddamn Rambo T-shirt?"

"Schwarzenegger in his best commando pose."

"Close enough. What about the earring?"

"No earrings, but Crackerjack diamonds on just about
every finger."

"Think he's one of our death squad dudes?"

"How would I know?" Lyons shot back. "Ann-Marie
was lying through her teeth. There wasn't any guy in a red

Rambo T-shirt, Gadgets. It's just coincidence that we happened across this character selling crack off some side street in downtown El Paso."

"What made *you* Mr. Know-it-all?" Schwarz challenged.

"Too many years wearing an LAPD badge," Ironman snarled. "On that job, gentlemen, you meet lots of lonely women...."

"I'll bet," Blancanales said, chuckling. "Must have been nice, Ironman, having a job like that. I hear most cops never sit home alone on a Saturday night."

"What's Diamond Rings doing now?" Schwarz asked, changing the subject.

"Absolutely nothing—just taking in the scenery."

"So what do *we* do now?"

"We wait."

Gadgets Schwarz sat back on his haunches and removed the latest rolled-up issue of *Popular Science* from his back pocket. He browsed through a few pages without really comprehending what his eyes scanned. "I hate waiting," he said finally.

A beat-up black three-quarter-ton truck eventually coasted up in front of the young man wearing the red T-shirt. At least a dozen Hispanic males wearing grubby clothes sat in the back. All of the men looked uneasy, as if they expected to see the INS agents from Immigration at any time.

"Illegal aliens don't make enough to snort coke, do they?" Blancanales asked, sounding bored.

"Maybe their driver does," Lyons responded guardedly.

The black truck blocked their view for a full five minutes, but none of the men of Able Team was concerned enough to exit the van and circle around for a closer look. When the vehicle finally pulled away, the vendor's wagon was closed and padlocked with a thick chain to the nearest concrete light standard. Diamond Rings was nowhere to be seen. He had evidently jumped into the truck, which coasted down the street now at a modest, unhurried speed.

"So what do we do *now*?" Schwarz challenged.

Lyons had moved up to the driver's seat. "As soon as the truck gets a little bit farther down the road," he began, starting up the engine, "we swing around." Blancanales and Schwarz felt the van make a U-turn and coast up in front of the vendor's wagon. "And dust that padlock."

Nodding, Blancanales had already taken a small packet from a trunk in the back of the van. Inside was a small paintbrush, preservation strips and fingerprint powder. He jumped out of the van, gauged the truck's progress down the boulevard, then rushed over and lifted four perfect latents in less than a minute.

"Why?" Schwarz demanded.

"Just for the hell of it, Gadgets." Lyons sighed.

Blancanales jumped back into the van, and Ironman sped to catch up with the truck carrying what was probably a load of undocumented workers.

The truck was still proceeding slowly down Pierce Avenue, eastbound, toward the Fort Bliss military reservation. At Dyer Street its driver hung a left, rolled down through a dead-end street and pulled up to what appeared to be an abandoned warehouse beneath the Freeway 54 overpass.

Expertly Lyons swerved in behind a dumpster and killed the engine as four of the men jumped from the truck and pushed back two sliding wooden access doors.

Exhaust pipe smoking, the truck lurched into the dark structure and disappeared until red brake lights appeared several feet inside. By then the workers had almost rolled the doors shut again.

"What do we do now?" Schwarz asked the man sitting stone-faced behind the steering wheel.

Lyons responded with a blank stare.

"I know the answer to this one," Gadgets said, slapping himself silly in mock rebuke. "We wait."

"Nope," Blancanales said, elbowing the electronics genius. "*You* wait."

"*We've* got a date with Ann-Marie," Ironman said, flashing a set of predatorlike teeth.

11

"Think we should have left him one of the CAR-15s?" Blancanales asked, glancing over at Lyons as they backed down the access road and returned to the main thoroughfare.

"Naw," Ironman said. "He'd stick out like Mike Tyson at a KKK rally—even back there. Gadget's handgun should suffice. Besides, he's got that portable radio you gave him. We'll be back to pick him up before anything goes down, anyway."

"I wish I was as sure about that as you," Rosario said as he stared out the passenger side window at the skeletons of several burned-out buildings. "What's this bullshit about going back to that woman's pad, anyway?"

"She was feedin' us one, Pol." Lyons's grin was a mixture of irritation at listening to her in the first place, and advanced satisfaction at the chewing-out he was planning on giving her. *If* she had remained in the run-down apartment after their initial "interview."

"Watch out!" Politician warned as two El Paso police cars roared through the intersection at high speed, emergency lights flashing but no sirens in operation. Lyons put the Bronco into a skid over to the side of the road.

"That was just a little too close for comfort," he said, wiping his brow. "Were they chasing someone?"

"Not unless he was the invisible man in a stealthmobile," Blancanales quipped.

"You should open for Rodney Dangerfield in Vegas, dude," the ex-cop said, coating his words with a mild layer of sarcasm.

"I'd get about as much respect as a jockstrap at a nudist convention," Blancanales told him seriously as his eyes followed the speeding patrol units, now several blocks distant. "Want to see what they're up to?" he asked, his chin jutting out in the direction of the squad cars as they disappeared around a corner half a mile away.

"I stopped chasing ambulances when I turned in my LAPD shield, chump."

"Probably just a no-account bar fight anyway."

"You're learning."

A static-filled voice suddenly crackled inside the glove compartment. "Dodge City to Alpha Tango-Two, over."

"What the hell!" Blancanales yelled, sitting bolt upright on his side of the van.

"In the glove compartment," Lyons said, motioning toward it. "Another portable radio."

"That was Brognola's voice."

"Well, open the damn glove compartment and talk to him!" Lyons reached over and popped the unlocked keyhole. The compartment fell open, revealing another handset which Politician grabbed.

"Alpha Tango-Two," he transmitted.

"Report to the airport at Fort Bliss, Pol," Brognola said. Both commandos could tell the connection was being fed into the radio waves via a telephone land line from several hundred, perhaps thousands of miles away.

"Roger," Blancanales replied. "Fort Bliss's airfield."

"An agent from the State Department will make himself known to you there. You're to be relayed to Houston, over."

"Confirm: Houston?" Blancanales asked, glancing over at his partner.

"Roger. As in Texas. Our suspects from the Assumption hit have struck again. Upon arrival you'll receive further instructions. Report ASAP, Pol—no dicking around. Got that?"

"Jesus," Blancanales said, shaking his head at Lyons. "Those bastards are really getting around."

"On the positive side, they haven't crossed the state line yet," Ironman said.

"Yeah. If the FBI gets into this, things will deteriorate fast." Into the radio mouthpiece, Blancanales said, "We're en route, Chief. Are you there now?"

"Negative. I'm airborne, passing over southern Belmopan at this—"

"Belmopan?" Blancanales repeated, locking eyes with Lyons again. "Where the hell is Belmopan?"

"Belize," came the simple answer.

"Uh, right." Blancanales remained slightly confused but didn't want to reveal he was unfamiliar with the Central American country.

"Brognola must be continuing on to El Salvador," Lyons reminded his partner.

"That explains it." Into the portable radio, Blancanales said, "Roger, Dodge City. We're en route. ETA three-zero. Keep us posted."

"You keep *me* posted, Politician," the Chief corrected Blancanales before signing off.

"What a killjoy," Rosario said, replacing the handset inside the glove compartment. "'No dicking around,' he says."

"I guess that means Ann-Marie will have to wait," Lyons added, staring straight ahead.

Blancanales didn't reply, and both men rode in silence for the half-hour ride to Fort Bliss. For the time being both near-legendary commandos exhibited a normal trait of human frailty—they completely forgot about Gadgets.

GADGETS SCHWARZ SCANNED the dark storm clouds gathering above the long row of abandoned warehouses straddling the western edge of El Paso's Freeway 54. The clouds reminded him of the monsoon thunderheads that could flatten an Asian ville in seconds, making life miserable for the villagers. One thing was clear: nothing was happening inside or outside of the warehouse, and if he stood around in the trees and bushes much longer, he was going to get drenched.

Glancing left, then right, he made sure no traffic was approaching. Pocketing the set of folding binoculars and turning off the portable radio's volume control, he sprinted from tree grove to tree grove, then into a wild hedgerow of shoulder-high bushes a stone's throw from the combination brick and cinder-block warehouse.

Pausing to check again for approaching automobiles or foot traffic, he drew his 9 mm Beretta 93-R and prepared to run up to the sliding dual-access doors that the workers' truck had passed through earlier.

The Beretta was equipped with a 20-round magazine and had been worth its weight in platinum in the past—*if* one could measure the value of one's life in terms of precious metals, he thought. The barrel was ventilated, the silencer customized to mask the earsplitting sound of any discharges.

There was only one window on the wall Schwarz was fast approaching with his quick run from cover. Barren of glass, the frame was covered with metal shutters and chicken wire. A chain-link fence, topped with sagging coils of razor-sharp barbed wire, jutted from either edge of the warehouse. Schwarz thought it might prove difficult to inspect the other walls for windows.

Not quite sure what he was looking for, Gadgets detected an upturned corner on one of the shutters when he reached the lone, unprotected window. Although he paused to listen for activity inside, he heard no movement whatsoever, other than a background hum from passing cars on the freeway a few hundred yards away. He slipped the Beretta back into its well-oiled leather holster and concentrated on calming his nerves. He preferred working this type of op using the team concept, but Lyons and Blancanales had, for all intents and purposes, abandoned him to his own devices. And Schwarz wasn't one to sit around and play rent-a-cop for anybody.

Lifting the portable radio to his lips, he switched off the squelch and turned up the volume until he could barely hear the hiss of static, then depressed the transmit lever. "Alpha Tango-Three to Alpha Tango-Two," he whispered into the radio.

There was no reply, and he knew from the manner in which static was now coming from the radio in weak sputters, instead of a steady hiss, that the battery was suffering a serious power drain. It probably hadn't been recharged in days. He had nobody but himself to blame for that.

"Alpha Tango-Three to Alpha Tango-Two" he repeated. This time there was no static whatsoever filling the radio network after he released the transmit lever.

The portable radio's battery was dead.

"Damn," he muttered under his breath.

Cautiously inserting his fingertips under the rusted shutter's edge, he flexed massive arm muscles, testing his reserves of strength then, satisfied, began prying the cover back.

That was when a twig snapped somewhere behind him, and the swirl of fight-or-flight adrenaline flooded his gut. But Schwarz had no time to do either. Someone had placed the barrel of a pistol against the base of his skull and pulled back the weapon's hammer with a sickening click.

12

Hal Brognola stared out the aircraft window at a small collection of huts, adobe villas and stucco dwellings scattered across a rare, barren patch of mesa near Gotera, El Salvador. The area had been the constant scene of violent clashes between Communist rebels and government troops for many years.

Now it was more peaceful. Leopoldo Vargas, former chief of the Salvadoran secret police, had returned to his place of birth.

The retired top cop had taken a platoon-strength contingent of specially trained commandos home with him. They had been assigned as the man's bodyguards. Permanently. For life. The *new* chief of the secret police saw to that. It was an unwritten rule. A matter of policy. Tradition. And besides, Vargas and he were old friends from way back. They had even attended a number of training academies in the United States together.

Vargas now lived on a sprawling fifty-acre plot of land an hour's drive, by Jeep, from Gotera—in the farming village of Lolotiquillo, six miles to the northeast. To get there one had to make a determined trek over terribly maintained roads, littered with the carcasses of cattle and the firebombed shells of old buses and transport trucks.

Vargas's property was ringed with three separate barbed wire fences, six guard towers and an intermittent series of concrete walls topped with embedded shards of broken glass. A moat, filled with deadly black water moccasins, meandered inside the fence line. The snakes were imported from Alabama, where Vargas had attended an eight-week mercenary survival camp a few months prior to retiring at he ripe young age of forty-eight.

Vargas had been a Salvadoran policeman for thirty years. He had put in his time and now he wanted to enjoy life. To Vargas, enjoyment meant relaxation. No more thrill-seeking on jungle patrols, tracking down guerrillas of the People's Revolutionary Army or FMLN. No more danger-seeking safaris hunting the big game of neighboring Honduras.

Vargas had amassed an eclectic but impressive library of American reference books and mystery novels over the past several years. He was ready for a good read, some serious research and several peaceful afternoons sipping tequila while he awaited the sunset. Vargas's next project would involve writing the great Salvadoran novel. It might not be a bestseller or make him rich, but it was something he had always wanted to do. Brick and concrete monuments to one's achievements were one thing, but they could collapse during an earthquake, or burn to the ground in a fire—Vargas had experienced both types of disaster in his lifetime. No, only the printed word offered the sense of immortality Vargas sought.

The financial success of the book was immaterial. Unlike places as notorious as Miami to the north—where goods and contraband seized from criminals were confiscated and utilized by the government for public auction later—police commanders in El Salvador were often allowed to keep many of the items their troops captured during narcotics raids or anticorruption stings. Not the drugs, of course. But a speedboat here or a trunkload of gold bars here were fair game. They were an incentive to improve police procedures and ensure the dedication and loyalty of one's men.

But today Vargas wasn't writing or relaxing in the sur
Today he was awaiting the arrival of a visitor from abroad
He checked his watch and scanned the skies through hi
blue-tinted shades, searching for that telltale speck tha
would warn him of the big man's arrival.

Unlike certain other law enforcers in Latin America
Vargas had conducted his official duties in an honest an
honorable manner. The tall, stocky Hispanic kept his hea
high and his long Zapata mustache immaculately trimmed
whether his daily activities included a public appearanc
before potential voters—he also had political aspira
tions—or a private dinner at the mayor's residence tw
miles away. He only wore the finest clothes and was neve
without his trademark U.S. Air Force fighter pilot sur
glasses and Army Cavalry riding boots—both gifts from hi
American friend, Hal Brognola. From time to time he als
wore a Colt .45 automatic on his hip. His Mark IV boaste
plain black Pachmyre grips and eight hollowpoints—on
always in the chamber, ready for action. The weapon ha
also been presented to him by Brognola some years prev
ously. It had been compliments of the U.S. Army's mil
tary police school at Fort McClellan, Alabama. The pisto
had a low serial number—three digits. Vargas often wor
dered if this had had something to do with Brognola's smil
that day, ten years earlier, but had decided not to ask.

There was no electricity or running water in Lolot
quillo. All drinking water had to be boiled. Even the wate
brought from the nearby waterfall that plummeted throug
a latticework terrace of cliffs below the Torola River had t
be carefully screened for contaminants, both natural an
man-made. It was also wise to inspect for crushed glass; th
guerrillas were well aware that the waterfall was Lolot
quillo's main source of drinking water. Many of the gue
rillas resided in Lolotiquillo by day and prowled th
countryside by night, ambushing any patrol of goverr

nent troops that ventured forth from its barracks in Gotera during the hours of darkness.

The villagers living in the tree-lined valley below the plateau on which Vargas's villa sat either burned gas lanterns or simply retired at dusk, rising again at dawn to toil in the fields or hike to Gotera for menial labor jobs. Vargas, of course, kept the perimeter of his property illuminated with the help of an American-made generator. It also powered his big-screen color TV set, VCR and satellite dish.

Normally his friend Brognola would have had to take one of the daily commercial flights from San Salvador, the capital, to San Miguel, the nation's third largest city. From there he'd board a smaller crop duster or helicopter to Gotera, and finally hire a Jeep north to Lolotiquillo, and trust the owner was no thief or bandit on the lookout for an easy *gringo* mark.

Brognola would have his own plane this time. Of that Vargas was convinced. And Vargas could accommodate him with a private airstrip immediately west of his villa on the pancake-flat plateau's edge overlooking the hillside villa where he and his five brothers and sisters had been born and raised.

All but Vargas now were dead, victims of crime, unforeseen disasters, war or a combination of all three. None of his siblings had died a natural death.

The retired police chief watched a dual-prop utility plane descend rapidly and bounce along the flat, sage-covered prairie runway five hundred yards away. When there were no incoming tracers to signal that guerrillas also awaited Hal Brognola, Vargas sauntered over to his Jeep and motioned the driver to proceed out to the taxiing aircraft.

"Welcome, welcome! *¿Qué pasa, amigo?*" he asked, holding a hand out to the big American after Brognola jumped from the aircraft's side door and climbed into the back of the Jeep. "What, no luggage, my friend?"

"Can't stay that long, *amigo*," Brognola said, his smi
seemingly tainted with grim purpose. This would be n
minivacation; there would be no mixing pleasure wit
business.

"But I've sent Pedro into Gotera for extra supplies,
Vargas said, laughing nonetheless. "You disappoint m
hombre. Still all work and no entertainment?"

"Perhaps later," Brognola said, winking as they pulle
up to the villa, where several heavily armed guards salute
Vargas as an iron grille gate coated with sagging strands
concertina was rolled back out of the way.

"Yes, perhaps later."

Once inside the villa, Brognola wasted no time briefin
Vargas about the incidents at both Assumption and Sai
Michael's.

"You understand, of course, that I no longer con
mand, in an official capacity, the officers assigned to wh
your news media delights in calling El Salvador's secr
police," Vargas said as he filled a glass with an unknow
liquor. Brognola had waved off the offer to join him in
drink.

"Don't call them *my* news media," the Stony Man chi
retorted.

"You know what I mean," Vargas argued as he walke
over to a glass-covered tabletop that held a collection
outlawed weapons confiscated from the local guerrillas
recent years. "Would you like an AK to take back with yo
Hal? They look great hanging on the wall of one's stud
you know."

"I've already got a couple framed and mounted back
D.C., pal. *Muchas gracias*. Now can we get down to bus
ness? I haven't got all day to pussyfoot around."

"Why so rushed?" Vargas asked, sipping from his glas
his expression remaining unruffled. "This is El Salvadc
my friend. The pace is not so frantic, not so rushed dov
in Central America. We have all the time in the free world

"The President himself is getting caught up in this, Leo. He refuses to believe the Salvadoran government would actually dispatch death squads across the border to silence outspoken political refugees from your—"

"Alleged political refugees," Vargas pointed out with a forefinger suddenly jutting from his glass.

"Call them whatever you want."

"I swear to you, my old friend," Vargas began, assuming an erect posture and holding his right hand up as if standing before a municipal judge and preparing to take an oath. "I know nothing about this El Playon Brigade of yours."

"Leo..."

Vargas waved the Stony Man chief silent. "Now if it was Mexican Brown you were asking about, or White Dragon Number Four, or even some in-transit Thai Buddha stick, then perhaps..."

"What?" Brognola asked, though he knew *exactly* what the retired police colonel was talking about.

"*Then* I might be able to assist you, Hal—if it is *dope* you were asking about, that is. Oh, I could tell you so much, my dear friend. There is a war raging down here over it, much more so than any fighting over politics or democracy or containing communism in Central America, I assure you."

Brognola leaned back and frowned. "You don't say."

"Oh, but I do. I must! Surely your colleagues in the DEA have mentioned the power struggle going on down here, what with the deaths last month of those two drug kingpins in Panama and Colombia. Accidental plane crash, my ass! Murder in the clouds, more like it."

"I leave dope to the DEA, Leo. Talk to me about death squads."

"Alleged death squads, Hal."

"Yes," Brognola said, turning to face the open-walled veranda. In the distance a pack of wild dogs raced across the horizon in pursuit of an antelope. "Well, the Presider is concerned that whoever's busting caps on the illegals going to eventually miss his mark and injure or kill inne cent Americans. Then the press corps *would* have a fie day over this fiasco. Perhaps you could...get word to the people involved that they should cool it for a while, a sume a low profile."

"I assure you, Hal," Vargas replied, walking over to the opposite side of the room where he lifted a framed gue rilla flag that was tattered by bullet holes. "None of m people are involved. And, as far as I know, none of the me assigned to the constabulary from which I recently retire even have the time, much less the desire, to raise hell nor of the border. What tactical support would they have? Vargas laughed. "It would be too dangerous...too risk But I will check into it further. How about an FMLN fl to take home with you?" he asked, pointing to the displa case. "It would impress the armchair commandos at the Pentagon, I'm sure."

"I'm sure," Brognola said, returning from the vera da's entryway without stepping outside. "But, thank yo no."

"As you wish."

"You've heard nothing of this group calling itself the Playon Brigade?" Brognola pressed.

"I have certainly heard of El Playon, my friend," Va gas said, his grin tightening. "I'm proud to say I con manded some of the troops responsible for filling the ma graves there."

"I know," Brognola said, fighting to keep an emotio less expression. "We've got telephoto pictures of almo everything that went on there. The death squads were ke very busy."

"Is it...*disgust* that I read in your eyes, my old friend? Vargas refilled his glass slowly, almost ceremoniously-pausing to wipe the imprint of his own lips from the edg taking time to recap the liquor bottle before replacing it in its slot on the shelf.

"Not disgust, Leo. No, not disgust."

Vargas tilted his head to one side slightly, perplexed. "Ah, yes," he said, laughing. "You regret having missed all the fun."

Brognola laughed along. "Something like that." But somehow he didn't sound sincere.

"For the first time," Vargas began as he moved to another display case, "I am unable to read your thoughts, my old friend. You, above all people schooled in these matters of jungle justice and the victors' vengeance, should know better. The press corps call them death squads. Well, I don't like those words. And let me explain something to you, something I'm positive you know well. This is a war zone. There are my people on the one side—the good guys, the soldiers and the government that is backed by the United States, no?"

"I'm listening," Brognola said, starting over toward the liquor cabinet.

"There's some Vietnamese *ba-muoi-ba* in there," Vargas said, his smile returning as he pointed toward the cabinet. "Made in Hong Kong, though, not Saigon. Spotted it on my last jaunt back to the Orient. Had a case shipped here. Took nine weeks to arrive, but does it matter? The stuff's lined with formaldehyde, right?"

"Right," Brognola said, chuckling. "I think I'll stick with the American brew," he decided, lifting a half-filled bottle of whiskey from its polished teakwood rack.

Vargas cleared his throat softly before taking another sip from his glass. "So," he said, "you agree that we are the good guys?"

"Of course."

"And that the Communist rebels and their sympathizers are the bad guys?"

"Yes."

"And that, as I said previously, El Salvador is currently classified as a war zone?"

"I would think so, based on the body count."

"And that, comparing your own experiences back in Vietnam, when the local peasants cooperated with the Vietcong in somewhat more than an intimidated capacity—such as manning lookout posts or tripping booby traps, or even constructing punji stake networks and tunnels to store ammo caches and perhaps an occasional underground VC field hospital—that this conduct would make them fair game in the ethics and morality aspects, or lack of same, associated with a free-fire zone?"

"You have an amusing way of putting things into perspective, Leo, of manipulating words to suit your purpose. You should be a politician," Brognola declared as he reached into his pocket and produced the black eagle patch recovered at the slaughter behind Assumption Church.

Vargas accepted the black patch with a smile. "It is similar to the patches worn by some of the free-lancers assigned to my old police battalion," he conceded. "I am talking about the eagle design. But El Playon Brigade is a fantasy, Hal. No such group, to my knowledge, exists."

Brognola's smile grew slightly. "Sanctioned, or nonsanctioned?"

"Sanctioned or nonsanctioned," Vargas said, nodding. "Not even in crazy El Salvador," he added with a dry chuckle. "Though retired, I am still bound to observe my country's secrecy laws. But I can tell you that we never organized, outfitted or authorized a so-called El Playon Brigade. Or anything even vaguely similar. Of course I make no apologies for the squads of men who *did* go out into the night and exterminate enemies of the state. That was war, Hal. It remains war. But the so-called death squads, whose activities have tapered down in recent years only because the number of Communist agents has decreased accordingly, are patriots, not scum—despite what your news media claims.

"But the battle is in El Salvador. If the troublemakers tire of the fight and the blood and the sacrifice and flee to North America, that is their prerogative. If their statements of condemnation toward my government bring the wrath of angry Salvadorans down on them, then so be it. I would think you might do better to check on a few of my fellow countrymen now residing in the United States," he said, snickering as he held the patch up to the light. "Because that's where this damn thing was made."

"What?" Brognola snatched the patch back for a closer inspection.

"Check the workmanship, the edges, my friend. Not even our finest military seamstresses produce patches of that quality. It was made north of the border. North of Mexico. It will be easy enough for you to confirm. The pattern of cross-stitching is most incriminating, if I may use that word."

Brognola mentally kicked himself for not covering that angle, checking such a possibility from the start. "You mean it might be possible that someone is trying to make the El Salvadoran military look bad by imitating a death squad's methods, coming up with this El Playon Brigade? I don't believe it for a moment. Too much trouble involved, too many innocents being killed."

"You yourself have worked in the psych-ops field, Hal," Vargas said, setting his glass down for the first time. "It is an old, often-used trick. Even the VC used it in Saigon. They'd dress up as South Vietnamese soldiers, then massacre a village of innocent civilians, except for one or two survivors. Survivors who would immediately blame the Saigon troops for the annihilation of their family and friends."

"It's not the same," Brognola countered. "These gunmen in Texas didn't terminate neutrals. They, if I'm to believe your theory, massacred over a dozen of their own people—Salvadorans sympathetic to their cause. Even priests leading the Sanctuary Movement.''

''As in Indochina, sacrifices must be made in time of war, Hal. There is a certain threshold that—''

''Nonsense. I refuse to believe it.''

''That is all well and fine,'' Vargas said, removing a glittering ceremonial dagger from yet another display case and presenting it, handle first, as an offering. But Brognola waved it away as his old friend continued speaking. ''But a man in your position should keep an open mind. Consider all the possibilities until you have concrete evidence, one way or the other.''

''That's a good suggestion,'' Brognola conceded. ''And I usually operate that way.'' He turned to face the veranda again, then produced a handkerchief and dabbed at the beads of perspiration lining his forehead. ''Must be this heat.''

''Yes,'' Vargas said, nodding. ''A curse of the tropics.''

Brognola checked his watch and stared through the bamboo bead curtains at the two men guarding the airplane that sat on Vargas's private runway a half mile distant. ''I was hoping to spend a few hours in San Salvador,'' he revealed. ''Talk to police commanders still on active duty, get their input. With you as an escort, of course.''

''I'm afraid you would be wasting your time,'' Vargas said, one of his eyebrows raising slightly as the crackle of sporadic rifle fire several hundred yards distant reached his ears. ''I am being honest with you. They would be privy to little more information about ongoing programs of neutralization than myself. I haven't been retired *that* long, you know.''

Brognola moved out onto the veranda this time. It was a forty-foot porch, in actuality, that extended along the villa's south wall, overlooking the plateau's edge. Constructed of thick wooden planks and protective chicken wire—to keep out hand-thrown grenades—it was also covered by an intricately woven thatch of palm fronds.

"But I will certainly do some checking on my own," Vargas said as he followed Brognola outside. "Everyone owes me favors. I will put out the collection plate and let you know."

"Shit," Brognola muttered as his eyes locked onto the plane that had brought him to the villa. Kissinger and Grimaldi were crouching behind the craft's wheel wells as a force of forty or fifty guerrillas, a hundred or so yards off, moved toward them, firing rifles and pistols.

Vargas rushed over toward a field phone hanging on the wall and instructed his perimeter guards to begin laying a fusillade of cover fire between the plane and the force of advancing guerrillas. At the same moment, mortar shells began walking toward the parked aircraft from the opposite direction.

"Let's go!" the Stony Man chief yelled, starting for the nearest heavily reinforced screen door as the din of weapons discharges reached a dull crescendo in the distance.

A sharp whistle split several strands of nearby chicken wire, and Vargas responded with a grunt. Brognola whirled at the sound of his friend's heavy body striking the wooden planks. He found Vargas facedown on the floor, right arm twitching as a pool of blood began spreading beneath his upper torso.

Brognola crouched, then speed-crawled over to Vargas's body as several more of the unseen sniper's bullets slammed into the veranda, ricocheting around with loud whistles as they struck iron support beams or the protective window grilles.

Brognola cautiously turned Vargas onto his side, expecting to find his old friend missing part of his face, but the retired police chief had sustained a gunshot wound to his right chest. The spasms had stopped, and the startled Salvadoran's eyes popped open, locking onto Brognola's.

"Ain't this a bitch?" he groaned as Hal removed his own safari shirt and applied direct pressure against the jagged wound.

"I think your lung has collapsed, *amigo*," Brognola muttered, ears cocked as they followed the sound of mortar shells landing in the distance. The string of falling projectiles was punctuated by the rolling concussion of an earthshaking blast.

One of the rounds had struck the plane.

He glanced over the edge of the veranda to confirm this and saw fireballs rising from the prop-driven craft, which had toppled over onto its side. There was no sign of Grimaldi or Kissinger. In the foreground several gun Jeeps, loaded down with Vargas's private militia, were rushing out to the hilltop landing strip as the guerrillas, deprived of their aeronautical prize by poor battlefield strategy and an overzealous mortar team, began scattering for opposite tree lines.

"At least the bastard didn't get me in the head," Vargas wheezed as blood bubbled out along the corners of his mouth. "Or the heart." He managed to tap his own wound with an inverted thumb. "I've been through this shit before," he said, forcing a smile when Brognola finally looked down at him again. "No problem."

"Can we land line for a chopper to get you to a hospital?"

"Those guerrillas have been crawling around out there all morning," Vargas said.

"What?" Brognola demanded.

"I didn't want to alarm you, old friend, but our commo with Gotera and the capital was cut shortly after I received your message that you were en route."

"Didn't want to alarm me, my ass," Brognola said, shaking his head. "You just didn't want to have to admit that the Commies severed your last link with the outside world. Think you'll be able to handle a Jeep ride back into

Gotera?" Brognola asked. "I think that mortar attack pretty well chewed up your runway out there. Not much chance of a Medevac getting in here."

Vargas's eyes fluttered. "No sweat. What about your men?"

"If they survived that initial skirmish, they'll be okay. The bad guys are rabbiting. It appears some of your gun Jeeps are en route for a mop-up operation."

"Good. Let's go and get it over with. I have a date with a pretty *señorita* tonight, Hal. I told her to bring along her seven sisters. You can have your choice. Hell, you can have two or three, if you can handle them." Vargas forced a hearty chuckle, and a fine crimson spray left his lips, settling over Brognola's bare chest.

"Damn," he growled, frowning at his longtime friend's condition. With the crackle of small-arms fire still sounding on the horizon, Brognola gently lifted Leopoldo Vargas off the floor and carried him outside into the creeping blanket of gunsmoke.

13

"On the ground, sucker."

Gadgets Schwarz didn't immediately comply. He recognized Border Patrolman Lanno's voice. But with the pistol barrel still planted firmly against the base of his skull, he wasn't sure if this was just a poorly timed joke or if the young INS agent was working with Able Team's elusive enemy on this case.

"You heard him, scum bag," another voice called out—Zamora's. "Spread-eagle in the mud, mister!"

And then Schwarz heard Patterson's dry laugh. They couldn't *all* be involved in a conspiracy.

Slowly Schwarz turned his head until he was looking into Lanno's unblinking eyes. He watched as Lanno lowered the lead sap handle he'd been brandishing like a pistol barrel and pocketed the persuader.

"I ought to deck your young ass," the Able Team commando threatened. But somehow Schwarz felt only slight pangs of anger in his belly. Perhaps they were diluted by the flood of relief he experienced at not having allowed one of the bad guys to get the drop on him after all. "But we'll call it even."

"He didn't splatter your brains all over the warehouse wall," Zamora said, chuckling, "and you didn't shit a brick."

For the first time Schwarz noticed that nearly a dozen additional agents were standing in the rain beside the roadway sixty or seventy yards away. They had arrived unnoticed. Schwarz's frown deepened. Was he finally beginning to lose his touch after all these years? Dismissing the notion, he decided that the din of raindrops falling on the warehouse roof had masked their arrival.

"We're here," Lanno said, "because some nosy passerby phoned in a complaint to El Paso's INS field office. Said that a bunch of wetbacks were cruising the area and had broken into an abandoned structure on warehouse row."

"And that there were three suspicious types loitering in a van nearby," Zamora added quickly.

"Real funny," Gadgets said, although he wasn't laughing.

"So here we are doing our duty," Patterson added. "Checking it out."

"Actually," Lanno said, ending the game. "*We're* here—" his thumb tapping his own chest and Zamora's "because your buddies, Lyons and Blancanales, forgot all about your no-account ass. From Fort Bliss they requested that we come over here and offer you a lift back to the Border Patrol barracks or that flea-trap motel—your choice."

"Where *are* Carl and Rosario?"

"Houston," Lanno said, smirking without further elaboration.

"Houston?"

"Yeah," Zamora said, shrugging. "Your boss diverted them up there on official business or some such secret shit."

"Then there really was no suspicious passerby?"

"Actually, there was. Some guy with a car phone up on the freeway overpass there. Coincidence, I suppose, but that was how we narrowed down your exact location."

"So are we going to raid this warehouse, or what?" Schwarz asked, getting anxious. "Though I'm sure anyone within a mile of here has already heard all this racket by now."

"Before we got here," Patterson informed Schwarz, "the RP phoned back to state that he saw the wetbacks exit through a rear door, hoof it over to that tree line—" he pointed beyond the long row of warehouses "—and pull some bikes up from a ditch before cruising over to a housing project in the barrio on the other side of the freeway."

"RP?"

"Reporting party."

"Oh . . ."

"That's official cop jargon," Lanno explained. "Forgot you're not Lyons."

"Not by a long shot," Schwarz said, feigning an insulted ego. "Well, I guess there's nothing much that can be accomplished here right now," he said, wiping the sweat from his brow with the back of his hand.

"So which will it be?" Zamora asked, motioning toward their Jeep. "Our place or yours?"

Gadgets grinned impishly. "Neither. Take me back to Assumption Church, will you?"

"Time to confess your sins, eh?" Lanno cracked.

Schwarz flashed a huge smile and gave his best Jimmy Carter impression. "Naw, time to do something about a little lady I met there," he said, a mental picture of Ann-Marie forming in his head.

"HOW BAD IS IT?"

"I'll survive," Cowboy Kissinger answered, shifting his six-two, two-hundred pound frame in the Land Rover's front seat until he could look back at Brognola. "Flesh wounds only serve to piss me off," he said, holding up the bandaged elbow for emphasis.

"Good," the Stony Man chief said, turning to the man seated beside him. "What about you, Jack? Wouldn't want to lose my ace pilot, that's for sure."

"I'm just glad we made it," Grimaldi said, staring out the window as he blew a purple gum bubble.

Brognola nodded, deciding not to press the matter. Instead, he stared out at an orange crescent moon shrouded in thunder clouds as it rode the horizon. Grimaldi had been known to respond to even life-threatening injuries with a crude joke or two instead of complaints. He had escaped the Communist attack unscathed, but he wasn't his usual wisecracking self. And that worried Brognola. Perhaps it was the oppressively hot climate—more muggy even than Vietnam, it seemed. Perhaps that was it. The heat had put a damper on Hal's attitude, as well.

"How much longer?" Kissinger asked their Salvadoran driver.

"Thirty minutes...maybe forty, *señor*" the police private answered, glancing up at his rearview mirror but refusing to lock eyes with the ex-DEA agent. Kissinger was Stony Man Farm's ace armorer and had accompanied Brognola on this short-notice jaunt south to Salvador because the Chief wanted two of his most trusted men aboard. They were, after all, entering a declared war zone.

As they rode in silence, Brognola thought back to the skirmish they'd survived a scant six hours ago.

Twenty-four guerrillas had been shot to death in the forests surrounding Vargas's plateau villa within thirty minutes after Brognola had successfully gotten the retired police chief to a government helipad in Gotera. From there it had been a short chopper ride to San Salvador and a military hospital where Vargas would receive the best ICU treatment south of Miami.

He had never lost consciousness, and before Brognola and his men had left, en route to the airport for a charter flight back to the States, Vargas had again assured the big Fed that he would check into this new angle involving the possibility that Salvadoran death squads were penetrating the U.S.

Now Jack Grimaldi's mood seemed to change for the better once they were in sight of a steady stream of cargo aircraft rising and descending at San Salvador's small but busy airport. A blue-and-white control tower beacon sent bright, pulsing shafts of light into the murky sky every few seconds. Red and green navigational lights ascended and dropped as smaller aircraft made abrupt landings, hoping to avoid rebel ground fire that occasionally originated in the hills rising along the outskirts of the airfields. "Maybe we should stay the night," he told Hal. "I *love* to eat boiled shrimp and steamed rice at an open-air café in a city at war."

Brognola laughed. "No can do," he said instead. "Got to get back to D.C., and report to the Man."

"The President himself?" Cowboy Kissinger said, cocking an eyebrow. No matter how long he'd been in this line of work, the thought that his boss actually drank coffee with the President still amazed him.

"Yep. He wants this death squad business terminated immediately. Anyway—" Brognola was cut off in midsentence as two brown taxis raced up on either side of the Land Rover.

"What the hell?" Cowboy exclaimed, sensing imminent trouble.

They were cruising down one of the airport's narrow but paved access roads that was usually reserved for military or police traffic. The fact that a taxi with no uniformed passengers in evidence was trying to pass them was a definite warning sign. That *two* cabs were involved signaled that something was very wrong.

Brognola dismissed the premonition of a kidnapping-in-progress when passengers in the back seats of both sedans suddenly leaned out the windows closest to the Land Rover. They held double-barreled shotguns. Cancel the kidnapping.

This was obviously a hit.

"Shit!" Kissinger was in the process of drawing the .45 he kept in a shoulder holster when their driver, true to his evasive tactics training, stomped both boots down on the brake pedal. The Land Rover's front end dipped nearly to the ground as its tires locked. Screeching rubber filled everyone's ears as the two cabs zoomed past, both 12-gauge discharges overshooting by a good thirty or forty feet.

"Way to go!" Grimaldi yelled, pulling a snub-nosed .38 from its ankle holster as they watched the cabs' rear seat gunmen fill one another with double-aught buckshot. He leaned out his window and popped off four rounds, knocking out the back window of one cab. The ace pilot then proceeded to reload the short-barreled revolver despite the two bullets remaining in the cylinder.

Almost immediately the Land Rover's driver switched pedals, stomping down on the gas this time. The front bumper rose several inches as the rear end scraped pavement, sending sparks into the sticky night air.

One taxi swerved to the right, disappearing down into a ditch where it climbed the opposite bank in a cloud of billowing dust, only to lose traction and roll back onto its top, crushing the driver underneath as he was thrown out a side window.

The other cab skidded, fishtailed to the left and wrapped its chassis—and the three Salvadorans riding inside—around a concrete lamppost. Brognola shielded his face against the resulting spray of crimson as the Land Rover shot past, rear wheels still burning rubber.

The trouble wasn't over, however. Up ahead a checkpoint was crowded with Salvadoran guards brandishing automatic rifles. And behind the Land Rover several additional sets of headlights had appeared.

Brognola grabbed the driver's collar from behind. "You wouldn't be setting us up, would you, pal?"

"No, sir!" the Salvadoran responded quickly, staring into the reflection of Brognola's eyes in the rearview mirror. "I am Colonel Vargas's nephew, if that makes you believe me more. He wouldn't risk my life in this manner. Surely you know that. He is *family* oriented."

"Maybe!" Cowboy Kissinger growled. "Maybe not!"

The high-pitched explanation brought an involuntary laugh from Brognola, and he released the man.

"Who *were* those guys back there?" Grimaldi demanded. "In the taxis."

"I have no idea, sir!" the driver yelled back. "Maybe Communists."

"Communists!" Brognola roared sarcastically as he drew his pistol.

"Vargas set us up!" Kissinger said. "His nephew here's expendable."

Suddenly the Land Rover's rear window exploded. Shards of glass flew inward, and the Americans ducked as a burst of green tracer passed through, spiderwebbing the windshield on its way out between the front windshield wipers.

Glancing back at their pursuers, Brognola determined that they weren't official police or military vehicles. All three needed muffler jobs and weren't being driven professionally, but were swerving back and forth along both sides of the road. One car looked like a beat-up Thunderbird or Continental.

"The men up ahead at the roadblock," Brognola began, grabbing the driver's collar again to get his undivided attention, "can they be trusted?"

"Normally, sir, I would say yes," the driver replied, his voice rising several octaves. "But under these circumstances, your guess is as good as mine, sir."

Brognola surveyed their makeshift arsenal. It was seriously lacking heavy firepower: three handguns and the carbine stowed under the driver's front seat. He wagered the rifle's bore was clogged with spiderwebs. "We'll take our chances with the troops manning the roadblock," the Stony Man chief said.

Before they were halfway to the checkpoint, however, the rear end of the Land Rover rose off the ground several feet. There was a loud, earsplitting pop, and then the slapping of rubber against pavement as another burst of tracers roared through the shattered rear window.

"Blowout!" Grimaldi shouted as he quickly brushed pieces of hot, partially melted glass from his collar.

"They got one of the tires!" the driver said, as he fought to keep control of the Land Rover. It veered sideways, swinging around until the protesting rims on the left side collapsed, and the chassis raced backward down the roadway, gears screaming like a banshee. The driver stomped down repeatedly on the brake pedal, but it went all the way to the floorboards again and again. The stench of overheated brake shoes filled the vehicle.

"Hold on!" Brognola yelled, issuing what he felt might very well be his last command, but the Land Rover didn't explode after smashing into the concrete barriers that ringed the checkpoint. Instead, jarred by the impact, the front end rose off the ground. The vehicle flipped over onto its roof and teetered precariously on an upended oil drum that was filled with sand, before rolling over onto the passenger side as their pursuers skidded up to the scene.

If their pursuers weren't exactly good drivers, they certainly could shoot. A minimum of six machine guns erupted from side windows, peppering the antisapper barriers and what remained of the Land Rover's windows. But their brief show of proficiency with firearms also proved the gunmen's doom.

The police officers manning the roadblock waited for the first barrage of tracers to subside, then opened up on the sedans with M-60s and grenade launchers.

Instantly two of the cars exploded in blinding orange fireballs as their gas tanks were hit. Overhead a Huey gunship flared into a no-nonsense hover directly over the gun-men. The pilot obviously didn't want to endanger his people on the ground, and therefore refrained from un-leashing the rocket pods, but the chopper's nose cannon was soon burping a nonstop stream of high-explosive rounds down into the ring of flames where eight or nine guerrillas were already glowing a soft neon blue—human charcoal.

"Holy shit!" Grimaldi yelled into Kissinger's ear. "I thought we were dust in the wind for a minute there, brother!"

"What?" Cowboy demanded, cupping his ears. "I can't hear a word you're saying!"

The concussions had temporarily snatched their ability to hear, but that didn't stop the Americans from continuing to shout at each other as Salvadoran police gun Jeeps encircled the scene. The police surveyed the overturned Land Rover and its occupants with unmasked suspicion.

Brognola gave the driver a bear hug. "You okay, kid? You okay?"

The young Salvadoran read Brognola's lips. "Yes!" he screamed back, nose to nose with the chief. "I'm all right! Are *you* all right?"

"What did you say, kid?"

Kissinger and Grimaldi joined the two, making a small huddle as plumes of drifting smoke engulfed them and wandering spotlights from nearby guard towers lanced back and forth across the eerie scene. "I think your man Vargas is true-blue!" Cowboy shouted above the clamor of several additional helicopters darting into stationary hovers above the confusion on the ground. "Nobody would go to all this trouble just to take you out of the picture. They wouldn't sacrifice all these men just to make a point."

Hal Brognola still couldn't hear anything except the ringing in his ears, but he was thinking exactly the same thing.

14

Flames rose nearly a hundred feet into the night sky as the two-story structure burned to the ground amid a sea of flashing police and TV camera lights. A battalion of fire fighting equipment lay idle several blocks away, prevented from responding to the scene by intermittent bursts of machine gun fire that was still erupting from a corner room in the fifty-year-old mansion. Located at the corner of Rio Grande and Mountain Road on Albuquerque's west side, the old house had been a landmark of sorts. Tomorrow it would be front page news.

No other structures in the immediate vicinity were threatened by the fire, so the police commander in charge of the scene appeared content to let the flames and smoke flush out the radicals hiding inside.

"Who the hell let that camera crew past the roadblocks?" a silver-haired police captain with bushy sideburns and bloodshot eyes demanded as two SWAT teams zigzagged from tree to tree in the mansion's huge front yard, moving into position for an urban assault on the crumbling dwelling.

"I don't know, sir!" a young lieutenant blurted as Lyons and Blancanales conferred with the commander about tactics.

The captain exploded as another female TV reporter sprinted from the blanket of gunsmoke, her cameraman and sound crew in tow. "Well, there's not much we can do about it now!"

"Somebody's going to get hurt here tonight if you don't control those civilians," Lyons argued, gesturing toward the news crews.

"What do you want me to do?" the captain asked, raising both hands as a helicopter—dual spotlights swishing back and forth beneath its belly—appeared only a few feet above treetops ringing the property. "Declare martial law?"

"That would be nice," Blancanales quipped.

"One of yours?" Lyons questioned at the brightly painted gold-and-silver chopper.

"Hell, no!" the captain said, frowning. "Our birds are all PD-blue and deadlined for parts or repairs. See the big number painted across the Bell's snout? That's the TV channel they represent, sport!"

"Damn," Blancanales and Lyons both muttered.

"Look." The captain sighed. "Headquarters ordered me to extend every courtesy to you two guys. I don't know who the hell you are, or where the hell you come from, or what the hell this is all about. I just know that shots started ringing out in the night about the same time the Pentagon blitzed my office with priority-one telexes, warning of your arrival, and I don't need that kind of clandestine shit, boys. I'm too close to retirement."

"A short-timer, eh?" Blancanales said, forcing a tight grin.

"There it is," the captain agreed. "Call it anything you want, but, yeah, I'm so short I'd have to climb a stepladder to touch a grasshopper's rear end, and let me tell you—"

The three of them dropped to one knee behind a patrol car as another burst of bullets was fired from the corner room across the street.

"Pardon me," Lyons said, leaning out only slightly in front of the radio car's front fender before popping off six rapid-fire rounds from his Python. The Colt .357 boasted an eight-inch barrel with ventilated rib and magnaported 152 mm barrel. It delivered one hell of a wallop. They listened as all six rounds slammed through glass directly over the spot from where the automatic weapons fire had originated. "That ought to keep the scum lying low for a while."

"Not bad for fifty meters," the captain said quietly as Lyons flipped the revolver's cylinder open, dropped the smoking weapon into his left palm, ejected the spent cartridges, slammed a plastic speedloader into place and forced a half-dozen fresh bullets home before smoothly reclosing the cylinder. It shut with a well-lubed click, and Ironman's thumb gently pressed against one of the cylinder grooves until it turned slightly, falling into sync. The pistol was now locked solid.

Some curls were still floating up from the .357's blue-steel barrel when still another burst of Thompson .45 was sprayed over the deep, unmowed lawn in their direction.

"Guess they're not sleeping!" Blancanales yelled as the squad car lost both headlights. Two tires opposite their position exploded, and the chassis listed to one side like a sinking boat.

"Can I authorize my people to level that place now?" the captain asked, repeating his earlier request.

Lyons had been hoping to capture somebody alive this time around. It didn't appear that fate's plans corresponded with his own, however.

They had initially received the call regarding Albuquerque PD's armored car robbery while still at Fort Bliss's airfield, preparing to depart for Houston. The first accounts trickling out of the city involved conflicting stories: one had it that four Hispanic males had just gunned down a truck full of undocumented workers leaving a strawberry patch near the Riverside Canal, where Rio Grande Boulevard and Griego Road come together. But then the police frequencies had been jammed with additional broadcasts indicating that the same gang was responsible for pulling up to an armored car parked in front of a movie house and cold-bloodedly killing the guard before making off with nearly fifty-thousand dollars in cash.

Witnesses to the incident were claiming that the security officer never had a chance: two Mexicans emerged from a clump of bushes as he left the cinema manager's office, placed a .44 Magnum against the back of his skull and pulled the trigger. Twice.

There wasn't much of the guard's face left. His partner, locked inside the armored car with a radio that refused to transmit because they had parked in a dead zone, was still in a state of shock at Albuquerque General Hospital.

Dead zone, indeed, Lyons had decided. Red Lance needed funds to finance their revolution, or their Sanctuary Movement. And since Albuquerque was only a hop, skip and jump—or roughly 250 miles—up Interstate 25 from the Texas state line, Able Team attempted to make radio contact with Hal Brognola for permission to deviate slightly from their earlier plans.

Lyons soon learned that Brognola's plane was mysteriously missing, however—its emergency locator beacon had activated somewhere near the town of Gotera in northern El Salvador, then disappeared from the airwaves shortly thereafter.

Lyons notified Stony Man Farm, and Aaron "the Bear" Kurtzman, the wheelchair-bound computer wizard running the compound in the Chief's absence, assured Ironman he'd look into the matter. Bear didn't seem too concerned about Brognola's disappearance, however, and Lyons didn't have the time to question the ace commo specialist's evasive responses.

If anyone could raise Brognola on the radio, though, it was Kurtzman—Lyons had worked with the ex-commando long enough to know that.

For now he concentrated on the matter at hand—flushing out the terrorists hiding in the mansion on Mountain Road. The building's owner was vacationing with his wife in Europe. He was a respected doctor in the community and had no children. The man was above suspicion—a regular contributor to several charities, including the police department's youth boxing program. When the police captain told Lyons that it was also common knowledge that the doctor was apolitical, he and Blancanales both decided the mansion's owner probably knew nothing about the current situation.

"In other words," the young lieutenant crouching beside Blancanales said, "whoever's in there has been freeloading in the owner's absence."

"Sounds more like burglary and trespassing to me," the captain said. Glancing at Lyons and his partner, he quickly amended his comment. "Not to mention discharging firearms within city limits, of course."

"And damaging public property," the lieutenant added as additional fragments of glass fell from the squad car's broken headlights.

"What about assault with a deadly weapon? Assault on *police officers*?" Blancanales asked.

"Well, that's the basics of the case, of course," the captain said in a scholarly manner. "I was thinking about the additional charges we could use to pad the county summonses."

"What about IDs on these guys?" Lyons cut in. "Anybody have *any* idea who the hell they are?"

"They're not locals, that's for sure!" the lieutenant revealed. "My sergeant already ran an NCIC check on that truck of theirs sitting in the middle of the tennis court in the backyard."

"And?" Blancanales pressed for the results.

"It's hot. Stolen yesterday out of El Paso."

Blancanales and Lyons nodded at each other as the captain reached down to turn up the volume on the portable radio hanging from his belt. "It's for me," he said, frowning, as if the phone had just rung. "Go ahead, Blue Diamond Six," he spoke into the transmitter.

"We're in position, Captain," a voice only a few dozen feet away advised over the handset. "Snipe-Alpha's got a bead on two targets right now. Want us to cap 'em?"

"Stand by." The captain glanced at Lyons. "You both know, of course, that none of those guys inside that house plan on being captured alive."

Biting at his lower lip, Lyons glanced over at the growing flames that had already engulfed half the building. "All I can request is that you make every attempt to keep one of them alive so that we can get to the bottom of this," he said finally. "Even if we have to interrogate him on an ICU gurney with tubes and hoses coming out of every hole in his body."

"We'll use only the minimum amount of force necessary to effect the arrest," the captain said calmly. But as he was bringing the portable radio back to his lips, one of the gunmen unleashed a 30-round burst of green tracers at the long line of patrol cars parked bumper-to-bumper across the street from the mansion. He used a fanning, left-to-right motion. Dozens of windshields and sonic bars exploded as hot slivers of glowing lead smashed through them.

Somewhere an officer started groaning. Two sirens began screaming as their control consoles were riddled with bullet holes.

"That does it!" the captain yelled, grinding his teeth together as he raised the portable radio again. "Blue Diamond Six," he called the SWAT team commander. "Green light. Do you copy? *Green light!*"

"Roger, thanks," came a scratchy reply, but even before the transmission broke squelch, nearly a dozen high-powered rifles, operated by police marksmen positioned all around the mansion, opened up with deadly accuracy.

The immediate result wasn't what anyone, even Lyons, expected. A devastating explosion leveled the walls supporting the corner of the building that had yet to catch fire. A nonstop crackle of discharging machine gun fire—sounding like a thousand M-60s and cherry bomb firecrackers going off two and three at a time—filled the night air, drowning out all other activity or noise. Hundreds of red, green and white tracers roared up into the sky like a monstrous, out-of-control fireworks display. A rolling blast of black smoke and debris roared out from the huge house in all directions, upending several of the nearest police cars and totally destroying one TV van.

It took the Albuquerque fire department four hours to bring the ensuing blaze under control. The entire time singed and toasted hundred-dollar bills from the armored car robbery floated down from the heavens, creating a frenzy of activity for patrolmen trying to resecure the scene below. Several times additional lawmen had to be brought in to prevent looting and preserve evidence. Dense smoke lingered in the neighborhood for hours afterwards.

"They obviously had an enormous cache of weapons and ammo in there somewhere," the captain said.

Lyons attempted to ascertain if Able Team's missing mechanical genius, Hermann Schwarz, was making any progress on the case in Texas, but the police captain, who had earlier made all the radios available to the two strangers from D.C., was no longer so accommodating, now that half the residents on the west side were complaining of smoke inhalation. He had other things to worry about. And he couldn't quite get over the nagging suspicion that trouble had come to town on the coattails of these two men.

"Too bad Gadgets wasn't here to see this," Blancanales lamented. "This beats any ammo dump explosion I ever saw in Nam, Carl. Gadgets really missed one hell of a show."

"I'm sure he's making himself useful back in El Paso," Ironman said with a sly grin.

"Yeah, he's probably trying to hustle that cute Panamanian number we questioned earlier."

"*Our* Gadgets?" Lyons charged in mock rebuke. "No way, José."

"Yeah, *our* Gadgets. I wouldn't put it past him—typical musketeer when we bad cats are away for the day."

"Naw."

"Ha!" Blancanales challenged. "*You* sure wanted to go back and see her again, if I recall correctly," he said, jabbing a taunting forefinger. "What makes you think Gadgets is any different? She was gorgeous, *amigo*."

"I just wanted to *talk* to her," Lyons said, shaking his head in resignation as another secondary blast rattled the house's foundation and dual concussions shook the portable command post van they were both leaning against.

"Talk to her," Blancanales said, laughing. "Yeah, sure."

It was later determined that a number of illegal aliens—gunned down by the men who'd been holed up in the mansion—were political refugees from El Salvador. Patches bearing a black eagle and the name El Playon Brigade were found scattered at the shooting scene.

Able Team would never learn who the gunmen in the burning mansion were, what their purpose in Albuquerque was or their future plans. The destruction was so total, in fact, that no trace of the dead terrorists was ever found.

"To Panama."

Hermann Schwarz held his glass of red wine to Ann-Marie's. "To Panama," he whispered.

She took a quiet sip, then lowered her glass, leaned forward and kissed him gently on the tip of his nose. "Thank you."

"For what?" he asked, staring past her through the balcony's iron grille and out at the twinkling city lights.

"For being here." She sighed, resting her head against his chest. "I have been so lonely."

Schwarz watched a woman walking down the alley below. She was carrying a child in her arms. Ann-Marie's child. The woman was her best friend, Ann-Marie claimed. She had taken the baby away for the evening so that the two of them could be alone together.

Schwarz watched the woman start up the steps to an apartment building across the alley, and then disappear into the building's so-called lobby. He swallowed silently—swallowed the guilt churning in the pit of his gut. It wasn't often he took advantage of a situation like this. But Ann-Marie seemed quite receptive to romance—even from a virtual stranger, their earlier "interview" aside. And it had been a long while since his duties with Able Team had allowed him any time with a woman.

Schwarz had returned to the apartment that afternoon, carrying a dozen red roses for Ann-Marie and a stuffed teddy bear for her child. There had been no infant in the room when she'd answered the door on his first knock and invited him in, but after a short phone call—in which she'd spoken so rapidly in Spanish that he'd been unable to follow the conversation—a woman in her early forties had appeared at the door, baby boy in her arms. He'd met her best friend, learned that Ann-Marie's son often spent hours with the woman's other children, then excused the two of them and escorted Ann-Marie to a fancy open-air café several blocks down from Assumption Church.

That had been two hours ago. He had planned on taking her to a theater, but she had insisted they return to her apartment. Ann-Marie had explained that she had been saving a bottle of wine for a special occasion.

Schwarz had told her that Lyons and Blancanales were out of town on business, and Ann-Marie hadn't pressed him with questions on the subject. Instead, now she pressed slender fingers along his biceps and chest, located the shoulder holster and pistol and calmly removed both as if she was used to the nightly ritual of stripping her man of weapons. As the widow of a soldier, she probably *was* used to seeing guns around the house.

"I need to feel someone close to me," she whispered into his ear with hot breath and a deep accent as they reached the midway point of the bottle of wine. Her hand began working the buttons of his shirt and soon had it removed. He listened to mosquitoes droning somewhere nearby but didn't seem to care if they posed a threat.

Gadgets leaned closer to her as they sat on the balcony, counting falling stars. He draped an arm around her shoulder. "I need to feel someone close to me," she repeated. "But not like that." Ann-Marie rose gracefully, pulling him back into the room toward the bed.

Schwarz stared at the blue satin sheets as she set the bottle of wine on a nightstand. Turning her back to him, she switched on a small stereo, and an old Carly Simon cassette, vintage 1970, began playing. Gadgets recognized "That's the Way I've Always Heard It Should Be" as Ann-Marie's hand rose behind her back to undo the buttons on the peasant dress she was wearing.

It soon fell to the floor around her feet and he stared at the smooth outline of her body as she turned and sat on the bed. Her body beckoned to him as the music pounded at the muggy night air and sirens wailed somewhere miles away.

"Come here," she requested in a soft, almost pleading tone.

Schwarz stared at the upturned tips of her breasts as her arms rose to remove the jade clip holding her hair in an unflattering bun.

As the silky strands cascaded around her shoulders, he allowed his pants to fall to the floor and stepped toward the bed.

Afterward, while she was in the shower, he stood at the balcony, staring out again at the city lights. He wished for the first time in years that he could be done with it, turn in his credentials, say goodbye to Hal Brognola and Able Team forever. Hell, he could do any number of other jobs: private investigator, security consultant, pick from a multitude of electronics or mechanical careers. And come home every night to Ann-Marie...

No woman had ever made love to him like that before.

Setting up house in El Paso might not be so bad. It was a great city—despite the tragic chain of events that had brought Able Team to town. The kid might prove to be a problem, of course. He'd never really been good with children—just didn't seem to have the patience for them. And he feared he was getting too old to change his ways at this late stage of the nondomestic game. But perhaps it was time to make an exception.

In hopes of clearing his head, Gadgets walked over to Ann-Marie's bureau. He stared at his face in the mirror, moving nose to nose with the reflection, examining the bloodshot eyes, searching for answers, wondering if this Panamanian beauty had done more than just seduce him with a bottle of cheap Chianti.

Had she actually *bewitched* him?

"Naw," Schwarz muttered as he searched for something to concentrate on, something to help clear his head of the guilt, indecision and anxiety.

He picked up a magazine, but it was in Spanish. Lying beneath it was a photo album. Glancing over his shoulder—she was still basking in the hot water—he stole a peak at its contents.

It seemed innocent enough. There were many photos of Ann-Marie, but none of her family. No pictures of the baby, and that struck him as odd, but only for a moment. The snapshots were obviously four or five years old—taken back in Panama City. Poses at parties with girlfriends and handsome men, picnics along some riverbank, riding the porcelain horses of a carousel at a fair. Ann-Marie always smiling, yet her eyes were filled with the same blank emptiness each time. There was no sparkle in her expression at all. The smiles seemed plastic, contrived. They reminded him of a politician's practiced laugh, of a model's forced grin. Pull back the lips, clench the teeth perfectly...

Gadgets couldn't resist. He set the photo album aside and softly opened the top drawer to Ann-Marie's dresser. It was filled with a modest assortment of undergarments—bras and panties, mostly white, hardly sexy enough to warrant a second look—and he was about to close the drawer when he noticed the passport sticking out from under one of the bras. She hadn't done a very good job of hiding it, he decided—if that's what she even intended: the drawer *was* cluttered with bank passbooks and what appeared to be immigration papers, as well.

He picked up the passport and opened it. The blue-and-green seal on the inside cover bore the words: "Government of El Salvador."

Not Panama.

His heart began to race, and then it began to thump. There was a second passport lying beneath the first.

It was a different size and color and had been issued in Managua, Nicaragua. Home of the Sandinistas. Land of the Communist threat to Central America.

Both passports contained her picture—identical photographs, in fact—but the names listed were different.

One was Theresa Mondragon. On the other, Lydia Sanchez.

Neither bore the first or middle names Ann-Marie.

"Gadgets," he muttered under his breath, "you've done gone and stepped smack-dab into water buffalo shit again."

Returning the passports to the drawer, he went back to the nightstand and quietly placed one of the wineglasses into his satchel, then glanced over at the door. Pondering his next move, he rubbed at the stubble on his chin and stared at a clock on the wall. So what if she was a spy?

Still nude, he padded into the bathroom. Gadgets Schwarz wanted to share the shower before all the hot water ran out.

15

"We were sure worried about you, Chief!"

"Ain't that the everloving truth!" Lyons said, nodding along with Blancanales in an almost comical situation. "We were due for a little spending money last week, and *still* haven't received any."

"What do you do with your money?" Hal Brognola asked, producing a large roll of bills and peeling several C-notes free. "By the way, where's your third leg?" he questioned as he handed out the late pay.

"Gadgets?" Blancanales's expression turned guilty.

"Yeah," Brognola answered, distributing the money liberally without appearing to count it. "Does he want some cash or not?"

"I'll take his share," Blancanales blurted out when the Chief started to return the roll to an inner pocket of his sport coat.

"Make sure it gets to him," Brognola said, grinning for the first time as he parted with a dozen more hundreds.

"What about me?" Cowboy Kissinger asked, leaning across the aircraft's miniconference table in the main lounge.

"How's the elbow?" Brognola said, gesturing toward the bloodstained bandages wrapped around the huge weapons expert's arm.

"I'll be all right," Kissinger insisted. "I've been through worse."

"We were worried about you guys for a while," Lyons commented. "How was El Salvador? Bear told us the Commies blew up Jackster's C-12 bomber and just about canceled *all* your tickets."

"Something like that," Brognola said, motioning to the somewhat more luxurious accommodations aboard the Air Force Lear jet he had commandeered in Miami, shortly after leaving the Central American hot spot. "But this baby will do just fine, thank you—until we get back to the Farm and pick up the Corsair."

"We're headed in the wrong direction to be flying back to the Shenandoah Valley, boss," Blancanales said. "I was just up front shooting the shit with Grimaldi. He says we're headed for Tucson."

"And I forgot to bring my cowboy hat," Lyons moaned, glancing at Kissinger.

"Two of a kind," Cowboy said, shaking his head in resignation. "Do you two clowns attend comedian college together in your spare time or something?"

"Shit," Brognola complained over Rosario's revelation. "Can't anybody keep a secret around here?"

"What happened in Houston?" Lyons asked.

"The same thing that happened in New Mexico—just a different gang of shooters involved. The situation there's been sanitized. You're no longer needed."

"I *need* to be needed," Lyons said, feeling mischievous. "Loved and wanted as well. Houston's got some nice babes pumping the oil industry there, Chief. Hell, don't you know anything?"

"Same El Playon Brigade patches left at the scene?" Blancanales asked, dismissing Ironman's antics with a subtle glare.

"You guessed it," Brognola replied. "Now fill me in on just what exactly went down in Albuquerque. I heard you guys napalmed some old geezer's pad while he was out of the country on vacation."

"Not quite," Blancanales groaned. "*You* tell him about it, Carl. The memory brings on a particularly vicious migraine."

Lyons briefed the Chief regarding the incident in Albuquerque, but there wasn't much to tell. Arson investigators at the scene had finally located a few badly burned propaganda flyers littering the debris. They bore the El Playon Brigade logo, and the silver-haired police captain was convinced they were the same band of gunmen who had murdered a truckload of Salvadoran refugees less than an hour before they'd holed up in the mansion. It was still unclear just exactly who the shooters worked for—the propaganda leaflets were nothing more than rambling dialogues of anti-Communist rhetoric—or how far the network of so-called death squads extended across the country.

Brognola explained his visit to Colonel Vargas and the retired police chief's denial that the government of El Salvador had anything to do with assassination teams north of the border—free-lance or otherwise. Brognola revealed that he believed in his old friend's sincerity. But he also told them about the hit team that had intercepted their Land Rover at the San Salvador airport. He said he found it very odd that no one on the El Salvador national police force could identify even a single body of the dozen or so corpses left after he, Cowboy Kissinger, Jack Grimaldi and the thirty checkpoint guards had defended themselves. The gunmen had carried no passports or local identification. A fingerprints check would take weeks, if not months. Needless to say, none of the bad guys survived the confrontation. There was no one left to interrogate—which was one of Brognola's specialties. But he did know that in all his years managing clandestine offices and safehouses down in Central America, he had never before witnessed an Hispanic commando group display such selfless fervor to complete the mission. "Yep," he decided finally. "They had to be hyped on something other than ideological dogma, guys. More like opium or something."

"Maybe crack," Lyons offered. "Or PCP."

"They certainly exhibited the superhuman desire associated with the latter, Carl."

The Stony Man chief explained that the only clue left at the messy shoot-out scene was a single Cuban cigar. "And what kind of goddamn clue is that?" Brognola asked rhetorically.

As soon as he was assured that Colonel Leopoldo Vargas would survive his chest wound, Brognola had boarded a plane for Miami and transferred to the Lear jet for an express flight west to Arizona via New Mexico. This, after receiving top secret communications from the State Department that police and sheriff's deputies in Tucson had surrounded a house near Davis Air Force Base. Apparently a carload of Hispanics had forced their way past the female residents' helpless protests, following a high-speed chase through the narrow, winding streets surrounding Randolph Park. The pursuit was the result of an aggravated assault in which the Mexicans allegedly ambushed several Salvadoran refugees leaving church services nearby. The crisis had rapidly deteriorated into a hostage situation.

The only thing left to do was hope that Able Team—or an American police agency somewhere—could come forward with a bona fide, living, breathing guerrilla with Salvadoran secret police tattoos on his chest or an El Playon Brigade patch in his pocket. Both highly unlikely.

Tucson might prove to be their last hope before this death squad business escalated into a nationwide epidemic of random gunfire and right-wing vigilante justice.

A blue Air Police sedan was waiting for them at Davis Air Force Base when the Lear jet touched down. Utilizing emergency lights and siren, the SP unit ferried Brognola's men to the barricade scene in less than five minutes.

The house on Palo Verde Road was a three-story white stucco affair with a sloping, red-tiled roof. The building was surrounded by huge oak trees, and the closest neighbor was four miles down the boulevard, although the area was far from rural in nature.

Dozens of Tucson police and Pima County sheriff's cars boasting various multicolored paint schemes encircled the building. A fleet of fire trucks and ambulances lined the street.

But there were no officers down on one knee behind cars aiming shotguns or assault rifles at the barricaded suspects. No SWAT teams scurrying into positions. No helicopters hovering nearby, ready to pounce if the bad guys attempted to flee out the back door.

Instead, everyone seemed to be milling about with almost casual indifference—the uneasy calm *after* the storm—watching a small group of uniformed men and women who were huddled around a black station wagon.

Brognola stared at the white letters emblazoned across the Cadillac's long side panel: Coroner.

"Don't tell me," the Stony Man chief groaned.

"All dead?" Lyons asked after stepping from the SP car and strolling over toward a reporter standing nearby. The elderly man, his crumpled hat angled down onto the brim of his nose to shade his eyes from the rising sun, scribbled viciously as his cameraman shot the six body bags lying in a crude semicircle on the lawn.

"Every last one of the guys," the reporter said, nodding grimly. "Got our own Jonestown here," he said.

"What?" Lyons questioned, stepping forward for a closer look. "You mean, mass suicide?"

"Yep," the reporter confirmed, not looking up from his yellow legal pad. "Single gunshot wound to the back of the head—behind the ear. Every last one of them. Just didn't want to be taken alive, I guess. Thought they were Pancho Villas or something."

Lyons glanced over at one of the Tucson sheriff's department's vans. It was filled with several sobbing college girls—tenants at the huge house, whose owner rented out rooms to students from the nearby campus. The gunmen had spared their lives. Lyons wondered if it was because the girls were American, not Salvadoran.

Brognola's shadow fell over Ironman. "Did you hear, Chief?"

"I heard," the boss from Stony Man Farm confirmed, staring down at the body bags as if he held a personal grudge against their presence. "Why is it a hardworking spook can't get an even break anymore these days?"

The reporter looked up for the first time, but the men from Able Team had already turned and started walking back toward the air policeman's smoking Plymouth.

This latest group of crazies hadn't been as thorough as other El Playon Brigade teams. Two shoe boxes filled with the black eagle patches, along with a wealth of revealing documents, were found in the vehicle they had abandoned at the scene.

The papers indicated that the teams of assassins were traveling to cities throughout the southwestern United States and would soon initiate a master plan of revenge on those who dared slander the fairly elected government of El Salvador.

Outspoken political refugees residing in havens previously thought to be safe from retribution would soon feel the wrath of El Playon. On American soil.

"There's no way we can get people to all of these places in time to do any good," Brognola said, his finger running down the hundred-plus cities listed in alphabetical order. "Even if we simply notified the local authorities and hoped their already overworked departments could provide the manpower necessary to intercept the hits, or simply frighten off the death squads with a show of strength."

"Highly unlikely," Lyons agreed. His eyes rose to greet the Air Force SP stepping from a second air police sedan that had just pulled up behind the unit used to ferry Able Team to the scene.

The security policeman in the blue beret handed Stony Man's chief a sealed packet. Inside were two simple sentences:

Simultaneous ambushes have just gone down in San Diego, Los Angeles, Phoenix, Santa Fe and Denver. Victims all outspoken political refugees from El Salvador, with El Playon Brigade patches nailed to their foreheads.

—Kurtzman

"From the Farm?" Lyons asked, lifting the decoded telex from Brognola's fingers.

"Afraid so."

"Where are we headed next?" Blancanales asked.

"Take your pick," Ironman answered, handing him the list of cities. "It's beginning to spread like the plague."

CLOAKED IN SHADOW, a faceless figure lifted an ivory pipe to his lips and inhaled deeply. He held the sweet fragrance deep inside his lungs for several moments as he stared down at the four men kneeling before him, their hands bound behind their backs, their heads bowed, eyes staring at the teak floorboards. Then he blew menacing smoke rings down at the trembling group.

A woman wearing only sheer silk pantaloons and silver slippers stood in a distant doorway, long black hair framing the outer edges of small but jutting breasts. Like the prisoners, her eyes were downcast, but her position at the entryway seemed to indicate that she wasn't being held against her will. She appeared to be Hispanic, with the high cheekbones and sloe eyes of Guatemalan royalty.

"Bring me another ball of opium!" the old man demanded. He cast his long pipe aside angrily, and the woman disappeared into an outer corridor. The man spoke in English, as if the language's sharp-tongued sounds pleased him, but his accent was Mexican. Two burly guards, sporting AK-47 rifles in a port arms position against their chests, resisted the urge to follow the shapely woman as she disappeared down the long hallway. Instead, they kept their eyes locked on the unmoving prisoners.

A young man wearing a white safari suit entered from the side door. In his early twenties, his features were partially obscured by a drooping hat once favored by plantation owners but now worn by few men in Latin America. He glanced at the prisoners with visible contempt and kicked out at the closest, striking a shin.

The prisoner winced but remained silent.

"Remove their bonds, René" the old man seated across from the group commanded.

"But El Robles," the young newcomer started to protest, "I don't advise—"

"They won't make a move," the old man said, laughing as if it were a welcome challenge. "Hector and his boyfriend would cut them to pieces. Right, Hector?"

The larger guard bowed slightly with an impressive grunt.

The man known as El Robles rose from his narcotics-financed seat of power in the expensively furnished anteroom and approached a large map of the world mounted on one wall. His forefinger roamed the United States, finally tapping the Texan cities of Houston and El Paso. "Which town is next?" he asked the young man.

"I thought we would try a two-pronged strike this time," the confident cartel lieutenant responded without hesitation. "Along the Texas–New Mexico border—Las Cruces to the north, El Paso to the south, sir."

"El Paso," the old man said, tapping the map again. "Didn't we already hit El Paso?"

"Three times. But Red Lance infests the area. Señora Sanchez has advised us that there is still considerable activity at Assumption Church. Using the Sanctuary Movement as a front, the Red Lance radicals seem to be expanding their network of clientele despite the hits. Their drug traffic has increased to the point that it is fast becoming a threat to our operations in the area. Frankly the competition is killing us, El Robles."

The old man seemed intrigued by something else. "Señora Sanchez?" he questioned, his eyebrows coming together suspiciously.

"You know her as Miss Mondragon, sir."

"Ah, yes..." A smile creased El Robles's weathered features. "Miss Mondragon with the beauty queen body."

"That's the one. She's become quite indispensable."

"Keep an eye on her, René," the old man said, his grin tightening into an odd twist.

"Sir?"

"A woman gifted with such charm and beauty can only get herself into trouble. It might compromise the organization."

"Yes, sir."

El Robles walked slowly over to a black marble table stacked high with expensive jewelry and music boxes. He lifted a laquerwood case from atop a felt-covered platter and removed a long-barreled dueling pistol from inside. Then he stepped over to the kneeling prisoners and tapped one on the shoulder.

"Y-yes, El Robles?" the man stammered, visibly shaken at being singled out.

"Adolfo. You screwed up, son."

"Yes, El Robles. I...I am so sorry, sir. I didn't mean to—"

"Your people in San Salvador botched the Vargas hit."

"Y-yes, El Robles, but the colonel proved more elusive and cunning than we expected," Adolfo said, glancing up for the first time, and the young man clad in white khaki rushed forward and slapped him. Adolfo's head dropped again, but his explanation continued. "And he was in the company of some bad *gringos* I never saw before, El Robles! Three who acted like Green Berets. I lost many men at the airport, and—"

"I am not interested in your excuses, Adolfo. Only in that you failed me. You failed the Great El Robles."

"Yes, Señor El Robles. I beg for your forgiveness, sir."

"It is not that easy!" the old man said, throwing his head back with an evil, unearthly laugh. "You cost me *money*!"

The old opium addict and peddler of China White, among other things, continued to chuckle as he turned to the map and ran his hand across the whole of Central America. "Mine," he said, laughing even more loudly this time. "All mine—Honduras, Guatemala, Costa Rica and most of Mexico. But El Salvador? No, not El Salvador!" He beat his fist against the blue star, indicating the main airport in that country's capital. "And why? *Why?*" He locked eyes with René. "Because of my old enemy, Leopoldo Vargas! That man has effectively smashed the largest illicit drug-running operation ever seen in his country. And he continues to plague me—despite the fact that he's retired! Tell me, does being a policeman carry a lifetime obligation, René?"

"I don't know, El Robles," the man in white said, lowering his eyes. "The police can be very...persistent. I've heard that this stubbornness, their dedication and love for the street, runs in their blood."

"One of my own people hit him!" Adolfo claimed. "Carlos here!" He indicated the man kneeling beside him. "Carlos managed to shoot him in the chest with a rifle! I saw the colonel fall with my own eyes, Señor El Robles!"

"But these Americans you speak of managed to save him," El Robles argued, rushing back to the prisoners and slapping the top of Carlos's head. "You made a grave error, Carlos! You can't even kill a man correctly!"

"I tried, El Robles! I swear, I—"

"Shut up!" the drug kingpin yelled, glancing to his left as the strikingly attractive woman reentered the anteroom. She was carrying a gold platter piled high with black balls of opium but, out of the mood, he waved her away. Head lowered, she backed out of the room and vanished.

"Proceed with the schedule," El Robles ordered, his tone announcing that the session was about to end. He indicated the wall map with a wave of his hand.

"Yes, sir," René said, bowing slightly. But he didn't leave. He sensed what was about to happen, and didn't want to miss the traditional ceremony.

El Robles stood before Carlos and grabbed the young man's chin, lifting him to his feet. "Today I grant you another life, Carlos!" He slapped the gunman viciously. "Do you feel that surge of renewed life rushing through your veins?"

"Yes . . . yes, El Robles! I feel it." Carlos nodded without any visible sign of anger in his features. He feared this man more than the wrath of God and was grateful to be spared, something he hadn't anticipated.

"Now get out!" El Robles hurled Carlos toward the exit, and a sentry escorted the exhilarated gunman from the room.

"But you, Adolfo," the old man said, his smile returning, "you have upset me, son. Botching the hit at San Salvador's airport. Allowing one of your people to shoot Colonel Vargas on the wrong side of the chest! Yes, you have really upset me, Adolfo."

Without further warning, El Robles raised the dueling pistol, placed the edge of the long barrel against Adolfo's forehead and calmly pulled the trigger.

Ears ringing from the deafening discharge, René winced as several drops of blood splashed back onto his white safari suit.

Blowing smoke from the barrel, El Robles slipped the pistol into his waistband and clapped his hands loudly, summoning the topless woman back into the room. "Bring the platter of opium back in here!" he commanded. "It is time for El Robles to relax, time to chase the dragon for a few hours."

16

"Begin with that slain priest over at Assumption Church," Brognola said, tapping his cigar butt on a wall-size map of the downtown area as they stood in the briefing room at El Paso police headquarters. "And see if you can track down Schwarz. Bear's been unable to raise him on the radio."

"You got it, Chief."

They spent the entire afternoon searching the halls and stairwells of the church, ignoring the protests of the priests who watched their every move. By sundown they found the secret panel in the basement rectory.

It led into a boiler room-type phone bank, similar to the one discovered at Saint Michael's. They were unable to locate additional chambers where illegal refugees could be harbored, but by nine o'clock Carl Lyons—with the aid of Patterson—managed to crack several of the Sanctuary Movement's computer passwords.

Blancanales had spent that time sifting through several padlocked trunks they'd found secreted inside a phony computer bank. "Check this little gem out," Pol finally exclaimed. He held up a cracked and yellowing FBI poster from the early seventies, bearing the undeniable likeness of the priest who had been killed outside Assumption Church. His real name was Joseph O'Hara. The charges against him included prison escape, drug trafficking, interstate shipment of controlled substances and child pornography. He was wanted by lawmen in ten different states.

"Guess he couldn't resist keeping the wanted poster for a souvenir," Patterson said.

"I'd do the same," Lyons said sarcastically. "How often does one make the FBI's top ten?"

"Shave off the beard," Blancanales observed. "add the white collar and voilà, instant Father Xavier."

"I like the name Joe O better," Lyons replied as he finally succeeded in bringing up a computer program he'd been working on for the past hour. "Damn straight!" he exclaimed, tapping a forefinger against the glowing green screen.

"What is it?" Patterson asked, leaning over his shoulder.

"Only a roster of every member of Red Lance."

"That Commie sympathizer bunch?" Patterson asked.

"We're still not sure just exactly who the hell they are," Blancanales explained. "But I'm beginning to get a gut feeling that this whole Sanctuary Movement is just a big front for something infinitely more evil."

"Such as?" Patterson asked, pulling up a chair.

"I can't put my finger on it yet, but if Red Lance really is just a bunch of old, burned-out hippies turned socialists, I'd wager they've turned to running drugs to pay their bills."

"Knocking off Salvadoran refugees in cities across the country doesn't quite strike me as being all that enlightened," Patterson said.

"Unless they're not refugees at all," Lyons said, smiling as the computer console beeped and another file replaced the roster. But he didn't elaborate on his cryptic remark.

"You've cracked a different directory," Blancanales said, matching his grin. "They look like addresses."

"Here's Saint Mikey's," Lyons said, his finger underlining the church's street address.

"And Assumption Church," Patterson pointed out.

"There are locations in several cities listed here," Lyons said as he quickly scanned several pages of data. "There's the shooting scene in Houston and the abandoned mansion they took over in Albuquerque."

"Wait a minute," Blancanales said. "Go back to El Paso. I want to see if that warehouse Gadgets was staking out is listed."

"No warehouse off Freeway 54," Lyons began as he quickly checked the numbers and street names. "But here's one we didn't know about, and it's outlined in bold letters." He glanced up at Patterson. "Any idea where that hundred block of Escobar Street is located?"

"Yep," Patterson confirmed, leaning back on his heels and folding massive forearms across a barrel chest. "On the south side of town, wrong side of the tracks. Right down the road from the Immigration office."

"How convenient," Blancanales said, his smile laced with anticipation.

"Let's go," Lyons said.

"Go where?" Politician asked, showing little enthusiasm for going out in the rain.

"I've got an awfully bad gut feeling about this thing," Lyons revealed. "Something tells me El Playon Brigade is going to strike again in El Paso, and strike soon. The house on Escobar's all we've got to go on right now."

"Sometimes you're a real pain in the ass, Ironman," Blancanales said, leaning back in a swivel chair and propping his boots on one of the computer consoles. "I was just getting comfortable."

"Well, get *un*comfortable," the ex-cop directed. "Landline the Chief and tell him we're en route to Escobar Street. Lock and load, mates. I'm hereby declaring a red alert in the big city tonight."

"Shit," Blancanales moaned. "Show the guy how to use a word processor and he thinks he can rule the world."

THE WINDOWS IN THE HOUSE on Escobar Street were dark. There was no activity whatsoever from midnight until 3:00 a.m.—foot traffic *or* vehicular. Only a light drizzle coated the slick roadway. Lyons, Blancanales, Patterson and two INS agents sat in the back of a beat-up Border Patrol van that was painted over a dull black and licensed with civilian plates.

"I think this is going to be a bust," Patterson complained after they had run out of coffee. "And I'm not talking arrests."

A few minutes after three, Lyons spotted the first sign of movement—down the street.

A Renegade Jeep, lights doused and engine off, coasted up behind the parked van. Inside were four smiling faces: Gadgets Schwarz and Agent Cooper, the Jeep's assigned operator, along with two additional patrolmen, Lanno and Zamora.

"El Paso headquarters advised us you were down here," Cooper said to Patterson with an open palm cupped against the gusts of wind now buffeting the neighborhood. "Any action?"

"Do you see any guests of the female persuasion present?" Blancanales cut in.

"Hold it!" Lyons said, raising a hand and demanding noise discipline as a station wagon appeared down the street. "Everybody down."

Heads lowered, they watched a carload of young Catholic nuns pull up to the target house, get out and quickly carry several dozen bags of groceries into the dwelling as sheets of heavy rain lashed at their black-and-white habits.

"Wonder where they got supplies at *this* time of night," Lyons said.

"There's a twenty-four-hour market half a mile away," Cooper told him.

"They sure eat a lot for penguins," Zamora quipped. "What's your belly tell you now, Carl?"

"My *gut* tells me there's a whole shit load of illegal aliens being housed and harbored inside there," Ironman answered, slapping his rock-hard stomach for emphasis.

"So what do we do now?" Lanno said. "Call in the cavalry for a good old-fashioned INS raid of the premises?"

"Negative," Lyons said, quickly holstering his enthusiasm. "We wait."

"We what?" Zamora and Cooper both asked.

"We watch for El Playon," Blancanales told them.

"The death squad dudes?" Patterson laughed softly. "We could be here all night. Hell, we could be here for *several* nights."

"You're free to leave anytime you want," Blancanales growled.

As the hours slowly passed, and the rain suddenly abated, it *did* seem like they would be there all night, that they were wasting their time.

When a predawn glow began to paint the eastern horizon in blue and pink pastels, six of the seven watchers were actually asleep. Carl Lyons plugged his ears against the cacophony of awful snores as he leaned back against the headrest. Soon his eyelids began to grow heavy and his head slowly drooped.

Despite what he was constantly claiming, Ironman was only human. By the time the blacked-out truck turned onto Escobar Street and began slowly cruising down the block toward them, Lyons had dozed off, too.

The men of Able Team nearly somersaulted backward over Patterson and his two border patrolmen when the explosions and automatic weapons fire erupted outside the van.

All eyes popped open, wide-awake, as several streams of glowing tracers ripped into the house across the street, destroying a huge picture window and blowing the doorframe and porch beams to pieces.

Lyons slowly brought the top of his head above the van's dashboard until he could clearly see the gunman's vehicle, parked only a few feet away, in the middle of the street, between Able Team and the house being fired on.

The four long-haired Mexicans standing in the back of the pickup truck all brandished AK-47 rifles. They wore jeans and T-shirts, but no uniforms. Rifle butts to their shoulders, they leaned into wild bursts, ignoring everything else on the block—the other residents, parked cars and porch lights flashing on.

Lyons watched as two of the riflemen emptied their ammo magazines with long, sustained bursts then calmly replaced the spent mags with fresh banana clips while their comrades continued to blast away on either side. Then the first two gunmen resumed firing again.

"We've got to do something!" Blancanales yelled. He finally located his CAR-15 and removed the dust balloon from around its flash suppressor.

"I agree, bro!" Lyons said, listening to the charging handle on Pol's assault rifle fly forward with a sharp clang as he climbed behind the driver's seat and reached for the ignition key. "But they're going to bolt on us!"

And he was right. Even before Ironman had finished his sentence, the truck's wheels began spinning. It lurched forward, nearly throwing three of the gunmen over the tailgate into the street, and started roaring off down the block.

Blancanales was already leaning out the van's passenger side window, spraying the truck's rear end with red tracers from his own rifle as a chorus of sirens rose in the distance.

Lyons gave Patterson and Cooper just enough time to jump out and run over to their Jeep. Then he threw the gearshift into first, ignoring the shower of lead that answered Politician's own savage barrage.

The van's windshield spiderwebbed, but he ignored the threat, popped the clutch and pulled in behind the truck as Blancanales and three of the startled gunmen began exchanging crazy bursts of glowing multicolored tracers.

The chase proceeded westbound along Escobar, running several dozen red lights and adding some thirty-seven El Paso patrol cars to the lights-and-sirens procession before it reached the on-ramp to U.S. Highway 180.

Lyons feared the truckload of riflemen would head south across the border, down into Mexico, but its driver surprised them all and proceeded in a northeasterly fashion, back through the city and along the southern boundaries of El Paso International Airport and Fort Bliss.

Once again Able Team found itself racing into the sun as the pursuit left downtown El Paso and roared across the rolling prairies and lush farmland outside the city.

"I think I made a mistake requesting the oldest van from the motor pool," Patterson said. He squatted behind the front seats as the long line of squad cars roared down the deserted four-lane highway, chasing after a Jeep, a van and a truck, in that order. Every red light on the van's dashboard was glowing, but the vehicle continued to keep up with the pickup truck, as its top speed wavered just under ninety miles per hour. "But I thought it would blend in better. Never thought this stakeout of yours would result in another chase."

"She's doing all right!" Blancanales answered as he reached forward and patted the van's dashboard. "How's the gas?"

"Full tank!" responded Lyons with a grin.

Many of the El Paso police units dropped out of the pursuit once it left the city limits, but some two dozen eager rookies and a couple of gung-ho types yet to earn that five-year star on their sleeves, and the mandatory mellowing out that came with it, willfully violated departmental policy. They continued the chase as several sheriffs' cars and state units joined the procession of flashing and blinking emergency lights winding its way through the towns of Hueco and Cornudas, heading for the Guadalupe Mountains National Park and the Texas–New Mexico border.

Glancing in his rearview mirror, Ironman's heart was warmed by the endless line of speeding lawmen braving possible reprimands, suspension or even job loss for remaining in the chase. Lifelong members of the Brotherhood of the Badge, they would refuse to allow the INS agents to pursue known felons out into the barren stretches of open space without proper backup. It was worth temporarily surrendering one's shield and a week or two of pay.

Up ahead the four gunmen lay in the bed of the truck, seeking cover from the occasional rifle bursts from Pol's CAR-15. One shot from the Mexicans, and the likelihood of a stray round striking one of the squad cars lined up behind the INS van increased tenfold, just by the sheer number of units participating in the pursuit.

With Texas's highest mountain, eighty-eight-hundred-foot Guadalupe Peak, rising through blankets of silver mist to the west, the high-speed caravan roared along winding stretches of wet highway, up steep slopes and down into majestic valleys until it finally crossed the New Mexico state line.

In the heart of Lincoln National Forest, five miles south of Whites City, a fleet of New Mexico state police cars joined the chase.

"Well, at least we've got plenty of backup!" Patterson yelled as the pickup truck swerved to the left, heading down a narrow access road that ran adjacent to Highway 11—the little known back road to a popular local natural wonder.

"I just wish I knew where the hell this bat-out-of-hell is headed!" Blancanales responded.

Lyons glanced at a wind-whipped sign suspended from shingles and flapping off to their left: Carlsbad Caverns National Park.

"This should prove interesting," he said, managing a dry laugh despite the numbing sensation invading his bone-white knuckles.

"I'm gettin' a terribly bad feeling about this, Lyons!" Patterson warned as they raced along the winding road, fast approaching the famous tourist attraction. "Something tells me those scum bags want to drive their truck into the biggest crowd of civilians they can find!"

Up ahead cars by the dozens were pulling off to the side of the road to allow the reckless pickup truck driver and endless line of police cars by. From a number of motor homes, gray-haired men and women leaned out side windows, attempting to capture the chase on videotape cameras. Someone waved a small American flag as the INS van raced past, followed by Cooper's Renegade and countless howling squad cars. Children cheered.

"Give it another try!" Ironman said, motioning toward Pol's CAR-15 with his chin as they suddenly reached a narrow stretch of hillside pavement devoid of tourists. "Bounce some bullets into his rear wheels, Pol! We've got to stop him before he rams that pickup into a busload of senior citizens!"

"I've already tried!" Blancanales argued. "But every time he sees me leaning out the window, he starts zigzagging back and forth. *You* saw him, Ironman!"

"Just keep shooting on rock and roll until you hit something!" Lyons insisted.

"Tunnel coming up!" Patterson pointed out as the Renegade attempted to pass them on the left, its sirens screaming as it pulled up beside the INS van.

Before reaching the tunnel, however, the pickup driver swerved off down a dirt road that suddenly appeared on the right between a break in the dense tree line.

Several patrol cars behind them—unable to negotiate the unexpected maneuver—continued on down the road as Lyons, Cooper and three or four Texas Ranger units managed. to stay with the suspects as they raced up a wooded hillside, then down into an unnaturally still and serene box canyon.

The road ended suddenly, giving way to a grassy meadow that seemed to end at a high cliff overlooking the Black River two or three hundred yards below. The truck skidded up to the bluff's edge, and Able Team temporarily lost sight of it in the ensuing cloud of swirling dust.

Warning bells clanging wildly inside his head were causing Carl Lyons's ears to ring as Patterson's shouts filled the crowded van. "Something's not right here, you guys! They're leading us into a trap!"

"So long as I don't see a thousand Indians on horseback lining the horizon like in a kill-the-Cavalry flick, I ain't gonna worry about it!" Ironman yelled back as his eyes darted around the terrain. "*Where'd* they go? *Where* the hell did they go?"

"Over there!" Blancanales said, pointing to the mouth of a cave partially visible at the foot of a heavily wooded hillside. Cooper's Renegade pulled up to the scene at that moment, dual electronic sirens still yelping, blue sonic bar flashing frantically. Behind them police cars began filling the box canyon like commuters mobbing Hong Kong's Star Ferry during rush hour.

Turning toward the cave, Lyons barely caught sight of one of the Mexicans' bobbing heads as he sprinted between some trees.

Blancanales was already off and running. He fired a burst of rifle shots from the hip, and the lawmen all heard a scream in the distance.

There were actually five naturally formed caves dotting the hillside that rose above the box canyon. The bluff and ridgeline that jutted out over the river valley offered a spectacular view, but it was an area not open to the public. That morning only pursued and pursuers intruded on the natural serenity of the forest's edge.

Blancanales and Lyons led the other lawmen toward the dense tree line jutting below the mouth of the nearest cave. They passed the dead Mexican—four or five rounds from Pol's deadly burst had nearly blown the man's entire head off from behind—and dropped into defensive crouches behind a cluster of towering spruce just as a shower of tracers erupted from several different positions along the hillside.

"Ambush!" Patterson shouted. He had taken a spare Able Team CAR-15 from its security locker in the van and, holding the rifle by the grip like a handgun, was shooting short bursts from right to left, then back again. "They're in the caves!"

And they were. At least a dozen men and women with AK-47s and Soviet SKSs lay behind green-and-blue limestone stalagmites in a classic last-man ambush. A number of officers chased after the sprinting pickup truck driver and his three surviving accomplices, only to be led into a trap in which the enemy outgunned them.

Until the remaining police officers involved in the interstate chase finally made their way down to the bluff, guided by the sound of all the shooting.

Carlsbad Caverns was world-famous for its huge underground catacombs and rock tunnels. Extending several hundred acres beneath the mountains of southeastern New Mexico, the colorful caves interconnected in an endless series of auditoriumlike chambers, many artificially illuminated by man until they resembled sacred cathedrals of nature. Thousands of tourists visited the park every year, trekking along dozens of miles of carefully inspected underworld trails in search of fossils, artifacts, subterranean creatures or simply the intense silence and peace that can only be found miles beneath the earth's surface. Hundreds of *other* miles' worth of horizontal shafts and deep pits along the park's outer fringes remained unlighted and off-limits to civilians, however. The majority of them had never been fully explored, and the state department of parks had declared the unlighted subterranean trails a hazardous danger to would-be adventurers.

The area accessed by these five cave openings was just such an area.

Ten minutes after Lyons and Patterson had the additional lawmen properly under cover behind tree trunks, boulders and cars, a bullhorn warning to surrender was given. It was promptly ignored, as was to be expected. Several dozen rounds of ammo were fired back at the officers in reply, actually. Shortly thereafter Ironman gave the hand signal, and hundreds of rifle and pistol rounds, issued by various police agencies across Texas and New Mexico, were efficiently discharged into the hillside's caverns.

Before they retreated deeper into the bowels of the earth, the Mexicans unleashed one last desperate fusillade of bullets at the policemen, and a white hot tracer, ricocheting off Patterson's belt buckle, lodged in a lifeless fig tree.

Smoke was soon billowing forth from the shriveled tree, and as Ironman led the others up the hillside in a rushing charge, the flames quickly spread to surrounding bushes and trees.

17

Banditos came before burning bark, however, and Able Team and the Texan lawmen charged toward the caves. While they struggled up through the sagebrush, cacti, tree branches and drifting wisps of forest fire smoke, half a dozen Texas Rangers remained behind, assuming sniper cover roles behind a couple of idling sheriffs' cars.

Their weapons expertise wasn't immediately needed.

Fourteen dead Mexicans of the so-called El Playon Brigade littered the mouths of each cave in various poses of ultimate liberation. The rest had retreated several hundred yards into the dark catacombs.

More sirens were winding down outside now as fire trucks from the nearby forest ranger's station began arriving. One of the Texas lawmen had radioed for them to help battle the tracer-ignited blaze that had already engulfed half the hillside and was sending probing fingers of glowing crimson down into several gullies, heading for the river valley.

"The answer to my prayers!" Lyons said out loud as he stood on the crystal-lined lip of one cave, silently rejoicing as blue smoke and brown dust rose all along the ridgeline in a tornadolike whirlwind. He watched as three New Mexico state police helicopters swooped down into a tentative hover over the box canyon's jutting bluff.

The Huey in the center flared in for a landing, crashing across several fire hoses that had already been laid down.

Two K-9 handlers jumped down over the landing skids. They controlled German Shepherds that strained against their leather leashes.

The police canines quickly led Able Team and their backup down the single tunnel all the Mexican gunmen had chosen for their apparent escape route. The dogs' arrival had saved precious time: there were six tunnels to choose from, with recent footprints in all of them. "Let's get to work!" Gadgets Schwarz ordered, switching his CAR-15 to full auto.

It soon became obvious that this isolated section of Carlsbad Caverns—well over a mile from the nearest stretch of catacombs open to the general public—was the permanent stateside headquarters of the El Playon Brigade. Booby traps were everywhere, as was evidence that the death squads had spent several hundred man-hours reinforcing certain cavern walls. The gunmen had made such a hasty retreat down into the dark, however, that they had managed to activate only two of the booby traps.

The police dogs proved that they were also skilled in this area of detection, sniffing out the trip wires and pressure devices long before any lawmen came in contact with them.

Searching with only five or six flashlights became quite unnerving. No one could find the switch to activate an electrical cord of lamps extending from the cave entrances to deep within the underground network, so they suspended lanterns from the cool rock ceiling every hundred yards or so for guidance.

Many were never lit, however. Intermittent bursts of rifle fire were still coming from the far end of the tunnel, and the men preferred to stalk their prey in total or near-total darkness rather than risk exposure to blinding tracers or hot lead.

Prowling in the pitch-black could become quite nerveracking, but the lawmen quickly adapted. They wanted these Mexicans badly. Blancanales wanted them more than most, but he experienced considerable difficulty with the manhunt: chasing the armed enemy down through the catacombs was strikingly similar to hunting Vietcong in the tunnels of Gia Dinh and Cho Gao, where he had lost many friends during the war. Biting his lower lip, he persevered, keeping less than a breath behind Lyons.

No sooner had they reached a monstrous cavern ringed by glowing stalagmites than a blinding blast sent Able Team and the police officers scurrying for cover behind the limestone outcroppings. The assassins of the El Playon Brigade had finally been backed into a corner. Like rats trapped on a sinking ship, they gathered together in a dead-end series of shafts and crevices and struck back with a vicious counterassault.

Lyons rarely carried more than seven banana clips—roughly two hundred rounds—for his CAR-15. He went through the entire supply of ammunition in less than five minutes as both sides exchanged an unending firestorm of flying lead.

Slowly, almost predictably, muzzle-flashes on the Mexican side decreased until there were only two men and two women holding out against the overwhelming number of police officers, who had suffered only a few minor injuries.

Finally, with Lyons and Blancanales directing the rate of fire at the surviving enemies' positions, endless streams of PD-blue tracer converged on the Mexicans until there was only one remaining.

She abandoned her rifle—it was now empty and useless—and rushed to climb a steep, sloping, jagged rock wall up to an escape tunnel no one else had noticed. In one last act of defiance against authority, she pulled out a handgun and fired it at the lawmen several times before continuing up the last few feet to the tunnel's opening.

In the blink of an eye over ten bullets slammed into her thighs, buttocks and lower back. A scream tore free from her throat, but none of the police officers heard it—their ears were still ringing from the previous underground gun battle.

Gadgets Schwarz watched her limp body, clad in black coveralls, roll down the limestone hillside. Semiconscious and groaning with shock, her battered and bloodied frame came to rest between two stalagmites that jutted up through the gloom and gunsmoke. He half expected the woman to be Ann-Marie.

Several of the lawmen rushed up to remove the .357 from her frozen fingers. Schwarz was among the first to reach her, and he was relieved to find she wasn't the woman he had shared a bottle of wine with one night in El Paso.

An enormous cache of weapons and explosives was found in the Brigade's underground hideaway. What the radicals were planning to do with the armament quickly became apparent after Lyons and the other lawmen located documents implicating a drug kingpin in Monterey, Mexico, as the gunmen's source of financial backing. That information also helped Blancanales understand why—since he'd first seen the riflemen at the shoot-out on Escobar Street—he'd felt they *were* Mexicans, and not Salvadoran secret police. Something in their faces...in their actions. Something about the coyotelike look in their eyes.

"There never was a death squad," Lyons told everyone. "Not in the purely political sense of the word, anyway. I've got a hunch these guys—and all the others who were shooting up Central American refugees from Houston to Los Angeles over the past week—were nothing more than hired thugs sent out by this El Robles character to knock off his competition. There was no political angle, no right-wing or left-wing conspiracy. I was suspicious ever since those guys in that pickup truck fired on some of the cop cars during the chase. You'd think so-called right-wing death squads would never draw down on the police, wouldn't you? I mean, aren't they supposed to be pro-law enforcement, government-sanctioned, and all that, if only under the table, so to speak.''

''But what about all the victims?'' Lanno pointed out. ''Are you going to tell me *they* were El Robles's competition, that they were all dope-runners, too? I refuse to believe it, man. I was there! I saw the stone-cold faces on some of the corpses.''

''You're right,'' Ironman conceded. ''But some of the priests in the Sanctuary Movement, and I'm just saying *some* of them, *were* narc godfathers. Hell, they weren't even priests, Lanno. We already proved that by unmasking Joe O'Hara, alias Father Xavier. Remember?''

''Then there was no Communist plot here?'' Zamora asked, rubbing at his temples, bewildered.

''Red Lance existed,'' Blancanales said. ''Regrettably it still exists. Their dogma is hard-core Marxist, but their pleasure is cold, hard cash. I think the easy money that came as a result of their financial schemes to build up the Red Lance empire simply corrupted them until they became closet hypocrites, placing the big buck ahead of their original socialist cause. They masqueraded as protectors of political refugees while they utilized the Sanctuary Movement cover to sell their dope to school children and the other innocents of America—citizens and illegals alike.''

''That's it in a nutshell,'' Lyons said, nodding. ''Basically.''

''And El Robles?'' Patterson asked.

''I'm sure we'll be able to find someone to take care of him,'' Schwarz answered, glancing first at Lyons, then Blancanales, who both nodded back somberly. He stared at two New Mexico state police officers carrying the wounded female guerrilla past on a stretcher. The only El Playon survivor of the underground shoot-out was a tough cookie and was still refusing to talk. The defiant look in her eyes as she was carried past made him think of Ann-Marie and their evening of wine and roses.... And the questions he'd posed afterward.

He reflected now on her explanations about the passports: that her dead husband—highly paranoid—had kept passports in different names from various countries for "protection" in case of emergencies.

Her reasoning that night had also reminded him of stories Carl had often told about his old undercover days with the LAPD, where they'd have the California Department of Motor Vehicles issue them multiple phony drivers' licenses bearing false names before hitting the streets on decoy duty. And Schwarz accepted her explanation because of Lyons's accounts. Life in Central America certainly forced some people to go to bizarre extremes to ensure their survival, as well.

That she was Panamanian and widowed at about the same time a drug kingpin from Panama City had died in a mysterious plane crash over Columbia was something he also wanted to put in the back of his mind. It was something he didn't wish to contemplate right now.

What was he worried about? She wasn't on any of the computer rosters found at the Red Lance boiler room beneath Assumption Church and he hadn't found any El Playon black eagle death squad patches in her purse, which had been a relief.

Schwarz decided his best option was to dismiss all previous suspicions about the woman, thank whichever deity was currently responsible for saving his unworthy butt yet another time and start over fresh. That decided, he returned his attention to the scene at hand and watched as INS Agents Cooper and Lanno moved toward him. Blancanales, Lyons and Patterson were still standing around the van that had led the chase for a hundred and fifty odd miles. Its engine now refused to turn over, and it appeared the beat-up Dodge would have to ride a tow back to El Paso.

"Your buddies and Patterson have bummed a ride back with a couple of Texas Rangers," Lanno told Gadgets. "Want to ride back with us in the Renegade?"

"Sure, but can you run me all the way down to Ann-Marie's apartment, *amigo*? You remember the place, don't you?"

"Of course. That housing project on McKelligon Road, the one that overlooks the massacre site behind the Church, right?"

"Right on," Schwarz said, wincing.

"No sweat, Gadgets."

"Anything back on that records check I asked for?"

"Nope. Computers been down because of last night's rain."

"How about that wineglass I asked you to check?"

"It's next in line at Forensics. Our lab boys have been quite busy lately, you know, ever since *you* clowns came to town."

"Yeah, well, keep me posted."

"You bet."

EPILOGUE

Hal Brognola leaned against the podium and stared down at the three exhausted men reclining in various uncomfortable positions on the folding metal chairs before him. Eyes closed, heads back, they didn't appear to be paying him any attention. But he'd continued the post-op briefing in the basement of El Paso's INS Headquarters, regardless. He knew they were listening. They always listened when the big Fed spoke.

"And that's about it," he ended, dusting off his hands as if washing them of the matter. "The Catholic archdiocese has agreed to cooperate in a federal investigation involving any priests active in the illegal Sanctuary Movement. They're also going to allow us to conduct background checks on any suspicious clergymen—to ensure they're not wanted by the FBI the way Joe O'Hara was."

"Were Fathers Franco and Felipe real priests?" Blancanales asked without losing the appearance that he was talking in his sleep.

"Far as we can tell," Brognola said. "Just misguided bleeding heart liberals caught up in this Sanctuary Movement mess."

"What about those two bozos from Saint Mikey's," Gadgets asked. "Cecilia and Francis, the hippy rejects who shot up the stairwell with an Uzi."

"They're on their way to a federal pen," Brognola replied. "Both were associates of Joe O'Hara. Both were wanted by the FBI—some type of involvement in the SDS back in the seventies. Bombed an Army recruiting station or something.''

''Wonderful,'' Schwarz said, sounding far from enthusiastic, however.

''What about the prints off the shell casing and the Volvo gas cap?'' Schwarz asked as he stood, wavering on his feet for a moment, then staggered over in the direction of a pay phone.

''Still no match.''

''Par for the course.''

''Can't have everything.'' Brognola sighed. ''Oh, and Gadgets!'' the Chief called after him. ''About this phone number you gave Bear to check on. It matches the one left by a Theresa on one of the answering machines confiscated at Saint Michael's. It's unlisted, which doesn't mean squat to us, of course. It's registered to an Emilio René Mondragon. Does that name mean anything to you?''

As he searched his pocket for change, Gadgets glanced back at Lyons and Blancanales. ''René? Isn't that a girl's name?''

Politician responded with a deadpan expression, ''Could go either way, sport.''

After the briefing, Gadgets phoned Ann-Marie's apartment. She answered on the first ring, sounding busy and agitated. She also sounded as if she was trying to avoid him, politely refusing repeated requests that he come over and see her in the next hour or so.

As was his nature, Gadgets persisted. ''I have a gift for your son,'' he claimed. ''A new teddy bear. And for you, my dear, an expensive bottle of wine. No Chianti. Only the best.''

''Well, all right,'' she finally relented. ''But not until eight o'clock tonight, okay? I've been spring cleaning all day. I'll need a few hours to get ready, okay?''

''Eight o'clock, it is, Ann-Marie.''

Being obnoxious wasn't one of Gadget's traits. He just happened to show up at her apartment two hours early. Timing was beyond his control. He couldn't wait to see her again.

The woman from Panama had bewitched the veteran commando.

Ann-Marie was obviously shocked to see him so soon. And it was also obvious to Gadgets that she had been planning to be long gone before he arrived at eight that night: the baby was nowhere to be found and the apartment was nearly empty of furniture. She was apparently moving out. All that remained were a few packing boxes, one nightstand and the bed.

He said nothing, however, preferring to let destiny take whatever course it had charted for him—good or bad. Police officers often suffer from the same malady. A good cop would then fall back on his training, doing whatever necessary to correct the situation, despite any protests of fate.

Gadgets closed the door behind him, locked it and poured two glasses of wine. Ann-Marie's attitude seemed to soften, and she became more carefree as the two of them slowly drained the wine bottle while listening to Latin pop music on a small radio, but she kept glancing at the wall clock.

After Gadgets returned from a visit to the bathroom, she seemed even more accommodating, offering to run down to the market and find him a decent meal, but Gadgets waved that suggestion aside. All he wanted tonight was her. All he needed was his Ann-Marie to weave her special brand of magic, soothing the mental wounds he'd received a mile beneath the earth in the dark bowels of New Mexico.

That request didn't seem to upset her, either. Smiling seductively, she turned down the light, disrobed and lay back on the bed, arms and legs shifting in the shadows provocatively, beckoning to him.

Gadgets's head began to swim as he stood and removed first his shirt, then his trousers. He briefly suspected that his drink had been tampered with, but quickly dismissed the silly notion when Ann-Marie reached out for him.

They made love beneath the twirling Casablanca-style ceiling fan, and Gadgets didn't remember collapsing across her chest, his mind dropping into a deep, dark abyss filled with a thousand fragmented faces of the woman they'd shot ten times inside the turquoise caves, the woman who had stared at him with icy, accusing eyes....

Gadgets woke to the sound of loud knocks at the door. Eyelids popping open, he locked onto the sight of Ann-Marie sitting upright across his hips, still nude, her hands raised high above her head, preparing to plunge a long, glittering dagger down into his heart.

Frozen with shock—he was unconvinced this wasn't just a bizarre twist to his weird string of nightmares—Gadgets stared into Ann-Marie's eyes as she straddled him, breasts swaying heavily, side to side, their firm slopes rising along with her arms and clasped hands, hands clasped around the long, gleaming blade of the five-hundred-year-old ceremonial dagger stolen from a sacred Aztec temple deep in the Mexican jungle.

A grizzly triangle of glowing holes suddenly appeared between her breasts as the door exploded inward and Lyons fired a burst of red tracers from the assault rifle held against his hip.

Ann-Marie flopped backward, her pelvis slipping from his as the bullets threw her off the bed, legs tangled together, arms bent back, bones snapping as she crashed awkwardly to the floor.

Slack-jawed and speechless, Gadgets stared at Carl Lyons for several moments. He noticed that Blancanales was at Ironman's side, Lanno and Zamora behind him. All three of them were holding pistols trained on the bed.

"A little birdie told us you might not be able to hold your liquor tonight, kid," Lyons said, producing a tense grin and displaying an FBI wanted poster with Ann-Marie's face plastered across the front of it.

The charges involved insurance fraud and planting explosives aboard an international airliner for the purpose of causing massive loss of life. In Bogotá.

"She's one of El Robles's women, Gadgets," Lyons added, shaking his head. "What you got, boy, a death wish or something?"

Schwarz just stared out through the sliding glass doors at the black iron grille that surrounded the balcony like a cage.

"The records check you requested is also back," Lanno said, laying the sheaf of computer hard copy on Gadgets's lap as Blancanales held a forefinger to Ann-Marie's throat, checking for a pulse.

The electronics wizard still sat on the edge of the bed, mesmerized by the sight of Ann-Marie lying on her back on the floor, limbs twisted beneath her body, rivulets of crimson running down the slopes of her breasts.

Lanno looked intently at Gadgets. "Her prints—the ones taken off that wineglass you gave me—match the latents lifted from the empty brass bullet cartridge and the Volvo gas cap. Yeah, she was firing down at the people right from her balcony that night O'Hara bought the farm."

"All this over drugs," Schwarz said, shaking his head in resignation. "When will it ever end?"

"You guys won this latest battle," Zamora said. "But we have to go after them at the top now. Not these penny-ante pushers who infest street corners. We have to go after the kingpins, Gadgets."

"No," Schwarz said as he stood up and walked out onto the balcony, ignoring Ann-Marie's open, unblinking eyes as they stared lifelessly up at the ceiling. "We have to target the users. Without demand the supply will eventually dry up.''

He stared down at a group of rowdy teenage girls clad in punker tights and heavy metal jackets, traversing the sidewalk below. ''We have to start with the children, teach them this crap is poison, that they have to avoid it the way they would a rattrap...or a rabid dog. The children are our only hope.''

''You're learning,'' Lyons said, locking eyes with Schwarz.

''Our only hope...'' Schwarz repeated as he turned back to stare into the night.

A ruthless mercenary threatens global stability.

DON PENDLETON's

MACK BOLAN.

BLOOD FEVER

A renegade mercenary calling himself the Major has been dealing in nuclear weapons manufactured with stolen technology and kidnapped scientists.

On a terrorist recon mission in Colorado, Bolan taps into the munitions dealer's global organization.

Now, one man's war against terrorism is about to put the death merchant out of business.

Available at your favorite retail outlet, or reserve your copy for shipping by sending your name, address, zip or postal code along with a check or money order for $4.70 (includes 75¢ for postage and handling) payable to Gold Eagle Books:

In the U.S.

Gold Eagle Books
901 Fuhrmann Blvd.
Box 1325
Buffalo, NY 14269-1325

In Canada

Gold Eagle Books
P.O. Box 609
Fort Erie, Ontario
L2A 5X3

Please specify book title with your order.

SB-17

**The past blew out in 2001.
Welcome to the future.**

JAMES AXLER
DEATH LANDS®
Northstar Rising

A generation after a global nuclear war, Minnesota is a
steamy tropical paradise of lush plants and horrifically mu-
tated insects. In this jungle, Ryan Cawdor and his band of
post-holocaust warriors uncover yet another freakish leg-
acy of a world gone hideously wrong: Vikings.

TAKE 'EM NOW

FOLDING SUNGLASSES
FROM GOLD EAGLE

Mean up your act with these tough, street-smart shades. Practical, too, because they fold 3 times into a handy, zip-up polyurethane pouch that fits neatly into your pocket. Rugged metal frame. Scratch-resistant acrylic lenses. Best of all, they can be yours for only $6.99.

MAIL YOUR ORDER TODAY.

Send your name, address, and zip code, along with a check or money order for just $6.99 + .75¢ for postage and handling (for a total of $7.74) payable to Gold Eagle Reader Service. (New York and Iowa residents please add applicable sales tax.)

Remove from pouch.

unfold once

GOLD EAGLE

Gold Eagle Reader Service
901 Fuhrmann Blvd.
P.O. Box 1396
Buffalo, N.Y. 14240-1396

unfold twice

and they're ready to wear

GES-1A

Offer not available in Canada.

"Able Team will go anywhere, do anything, in
order to complete their mission."
—*West Coast Review of Books*

MEAN STREETS

DICK STIVERS

The Desmondos, an organized street gang, are terrorizing the
streets of Los Angeles armed with AK-47s and full-auto Uzis.

Carl Lyons and his men are sent in to follow the trail of blood
and drugs to the power behind these teenage terrorists.

The Desmondos are bad, but they haven't met Able Team.